Literature for Life Series
General Editor: Kenyon Calthrop

MODERN SHORT STORIES IN ENGLISH

Selected and introduced by Barrie Wade

D1392699

Nelson

Thomas Nelson and Sons Ltd
Nelson House Mayfield Road
Walton-on-Thames Surrey
KT12 5PL UK

Thomas Nelson Australia
102 Dodds Street
South Melbourne
Victoria 3205 Australia

Nelson Canada
1120 Birchmount Road
Scarborough Ontario
M1K 5G4 Canada

© Barrie Wade 1980

First published by Arnold-Wheaton 1980
ISBN 0-08-024203-0

This edition published by Thomas Nelson and Sons Ltd 1992

I(T)P Thomas Nelson is an International
       Thomson Publishing Company

I(T)P is used under licence

ISBN 0-17-432277-1
NPN 9 8 7 6

Printed in China

Cover photograph by Martin Chambers

CONTENTS

ACKNOWLEDGEMENTS

For permission to reprint the stories included in this book, we are indebted to:

Curtis Brown Ltd and the Estate of Joyce Cary for Joyce Cary's 'Growing Up' from *Spring Song and Other Stories,* published by Michael Joseph Ltd; and to Curtis Brown Ltd and Doris Lessing for Doris Lessing's 'Through the Tunnel' from *The Habit of Loving,* published by MacGibbon & Kee Ltd

Jonathan Cape Ltd and the Executors of the Ernest Hemingway Estate for Ernest Hemingway's 'The End of Something' from *The First Forty-nine Stories;* and to Jonathan Cape Ltd and the Executors of the James Joyce Estate for James Joyce's 'Araby' from *The Dubliners*

Rosica Colin Ltd and Alan Sillitoe for 'The Disgrace of Jim Scarfedale', Copyright © Alan Sillitoe 1959, from *The Loneliness of the Long-distance Runner,* published by W. H. Allen Ltd

André Deutsch Ltd and Laurie Lee for 'The Opposite Sex', published as 'First Love' in *I Can't Stay Long*

Faber & Faber Ltd and Ted Hughes for 'Sunday' from *Wodwo*

David Higham Associates Ltd and the Trustees for the Copyrights of the late Dylan Thomas for Dylan Thomas's 'The Followers' from *A Prospect of the Sea,* published by J. M. Dent & Sons Ltd

Olwyn Hughes and Ted Hughes for Sylvia Plath's 'Superman and Paula Brown's New Snowsuit', Copyright © Ted Hughes 1977, from *Johnny Panic and the Bible of Dreams,* published by Harper & Row

A. D. Peters & Co. Ltd for Frank O'Connor's 'Pity' from *Stories of Frank O'Connor,* published by Hamish Hamilton Ltd

Laurence Pollinger Ltd and the Estate of the late H. E. Bates for H. E. Bates's 'Great Uncle Crow' from *The Watercress Girl and Other Stories,* published by Michael Joseph Ltd; and to Laurence Pollinger Ltd and William Saroyan for William Saroyan's 'The Parsley Garden' from *The Assyrian and Other Stories,* published by Faber & Faber Ltd

A.P. Watt Ltd and Sean O'Faolain for Sean O'Faolain's 'The Trout' from *Stories of Sean O'Faolain,* published by Penguin Books Ltd

INTRODUCTION

THIS collection of stories touches on aspects of growing up: it is arranged to follow a development through adolescence to adulthood. It provides a useful source of material for teachers and pupils wishing to look at aspects of the short story in English within the context of first examinations or as part of a broader study. Certainly there are some fascinating comparisons and contrasts to be made between the stories. The book will also be useful to classes studying in a wider context certain aspects of growing up. Others will simply enjoy the stories for their own sake as works of literature.

With a collection so very varied in style and treatment (as one would expect from such a wide range of authors) final classifications are difficult. However, in making the selection, I have had two criteria in mind. First, that the stories should appeal and give pleasure to pupils in the middle and upper levels of secondary schools. Secondly, since they deal with the complexity of experience, that they will repay close study. As an aid to this kind of study I have provided after each story a number of starting-points. Naturally teachers and classes will wish to supplement these with some of their own. The starting-points are designed to encourage rereading and reflection by pupils, so that they may avoid the sort of rush to judgement which comes through grabbing at other people's opinions, or tackling a story too soon on an abstract critical level.

These stories can *lead to* critical study, but the starting-points are intended to stimulate the important initial responses of understanding, experiencing and insight. Interpretation is a creative and active process in which the individual reader builds for himself the world that the writer has conceived, bringing to it such of his own experiences as can help him evaluate the themes of a story.

Interpreting the writer's world is an active process; it can also very profitably be a co-operative one. We can learn much from other people's responses and experiences as well as from our own. Many of the starting-points should stimulate open, exploratory discussions and co-operative activities. The stories presenting experiences different from or similar to those of the reader will allow him to reflect on them from a safe distance. They may also encourage his imaginative insight in contemplating the feelings and motivations of the characters.

Some of the starting-points include or lead naturally to a more reflective or creative response in writing. Others offer specific suggestions based on each story. At the end of the collection are examples of assignments that can be attempted when the majority of the stories have been studied.

In compiling this collection I have valued the chance to talk with colleagues and students, with advisers and examiners, and I acknowledge gratefully the help and advice I have received from more people than I can name here. I owe a particular debt of pleasure to those pupils in schools with whom I have explored these stories; I have learned a good deal from them.

Barrie Wade

SUNDAY

Ted Hughes

MICHAEL marched off to chapel beside his sister, rapping his Sunday shoes down on to the pavement to fetch the brisk, stinging echo off house walls, wearing the detestable blue blazer with its meaningless badge as a uniform loaded with honours and privilege. In chapel he sat erect, arms folded, instead of curling down on to his spine like a prawn and sinking his chin between his collar-bones as under the steady pressure of a great hand, which was his usual attitude of worship. He sang the hymns and during the prayers thought exultantly of Top Wharf Pub, trying to remember what time those places opened.

All this zest, however, was no match for the sermon. The minister's voice soared among the beams, tireless, as if he were still rehearsing, and after ten minutes these organ-like modulations began to work Michael into a torment of impatience. The nerve-ends all over his body prickled and swarmed. He almost had to sink to his knees. Thoughts of shouting 'Oh well!' – one enormous sigh, or simply running out of chapel, brought a fine sweat to his temples. Finally he closed his eyes and began to imagine a wolf galloping through snow-filled, moonlit forest. Without fail this image was the first thing in his mind whenever he shut his eyes on these situations of constraint, in school, in waiting-rooms, with visitors. The wolf urged itself with all its strength through a land empty of everything but trees and snow. After a while he drifted to vaguer things, a few moments of freedom before his impatience jerked him back to see how the sermon was doing. It was still soaring. He closed his eyes and the wolf was there again.

By the time the doors opened, letting light stream in, he felt stupefied. He edged out with the crowd. Then the eleven o'clock Sunday sky struck him. He had forgotten it was so early in the day. But with the light and the outside world his mind returned in a rush. Leaving his sister deep in the chapel, buried in a pink and blue

1

bouquet of her friends, and evading the minister who, having processed his congregation generally within, had darted round the side of the chapel to the porch and was now setting his personal seal, a crushing smile and a soft, supporting handclasp, on each member of the flock as they stumbled out, Michael took the three broad steps at a leap and dodged down the crowded path among the graves, like a person with an important dispatch.

But he was no sooner out through the gate than the stitches of his shoes seemed suddenly to tighten, and his damped hair tightened on his scalp. He slowed to a walk.

To the farthest skyline it was Sunday. The valley walls, throughout the week wet, hanging, uncomfortable woods and mud-hole farms, were today neat, remote and irreproachably pretty, postcard pretty. The blue sky, the sparklingly smokeless Sunday air, had disinfected them. Picnickers and chapel-hikers were already up there, sprinkled like confetti along the steep lanes and paths, creeping imperceptibly upward towards the brown line of the moors. Spotless, harmless, church-going slopes! Life, over the whole countryside, was suspended for the day.

Below him the town glittered in the clear air and sunlight. Throughout the week it resembled from this point a volcanic pit, bottomless in places, a jagged fissure into a sulphurous underworld, the smoke dragging off the chimneys of the mills and houserows like a tearing fleece. Now it lay as under shallow, slightly warm, clear water, with still streets and bright yards.

There was even something Sundayish about the pavements, something untouchably proper, though nothing had gone over them since grubby Saturday except more feet and darkness.

Superior to all this for once, and quite enjoying it again now he was on his way, Michael went down the hill into the town with strides that jammed his toes into the ends of his shoes. He turned into the Memorial Gardens, past prams, rockeries, forbidden grass, trees with labels, and over the ornamental canal bridge to the bowling-greens that lay on the level between canal and river.

His father was there, on the farthest green, with two familiar figures – Harry Rutley, the pork butcher, and Mr Stinson, a tall, sooty, lean man who held his head as if he were blind and spoke rarely, and then only as if phrasing his most private thoughts to himself. A man Michael preferred not to look at. Michael sat on a park bench behind their jack and tried to make himself obvious.

The paths were full of people. Last night this had been a parade of couples, foursomes, gangs and lonely ones – the electricity gathered off looms, sewing-machines and shop counters since Monday milling round the circuit and discharging up the sidepaths among the shrubbery in giggling darkness and shrieks. But now it was families, an after-chapel procession of rustlings and murmurings, lacy bosoms, tight blue pin-stripe suits and daisy-chains of children. Soon Michael was worn out, willing the bowls against their bias or against the crown of the green or to roll one foot farther and into the trough or to collide and fall in halves. He could see the Wesleyan Church clock at quarter past eleven and stared at it for what seemed like five minutes, convinced it had stopped.

He stood up as the three men came over to study the pattern of the bowls.

'Are we going now, Dad?'

'Just a minute, lad. Come and have a game.'

That meant at least another game whether he played or not. Another quarter of an hour! And to go and get out a pair of bowls was as good as agreeing to stay there playing till one.

'We might miss him.'

His father laughed. Only just remembering his promise, thought Michael.

'He'll not be there till well on. We shan't miss him.'

His father kicked his bowls together and Harry Rutley slewed the rubber mat into position.

'But will he be there sure?'

Sunday dinner was closer every minute. Then it was sleepy Sunday afternoon. Then Aunt-infested Sunday tea. His father laughed again.

'Billy Red'll be coming down today, won't he, Harry?'

Harry Rutley, pale, slow, round, weighed his jack. He had lost the tip of an ear at the Dardanelles and carried a fragment of his fifth rib on the end of his watch-chain. Now he narrowed his eyes, choosing a particular blade of grass on the far corner of the green.

'Billy Red? Every Sunday. Twelve on the dot.' He dipped his body to the underswing of his arm and came upright as the jack curled away across the green. 'I don't know how he does it.'

The jack had come to rest two feet from the far corner. There followed four more games. They played back to Michael, then across to the far right, then a short one down to the far left, then back to the near right. At last the green was too full, with nine or ten games interweaving and shouts of 'feet' every other minute and bowls bocking together in mid-green.

At quarter to twelve on the clock – Michael now sullen with the punishment he had undergone and the certainty that his day had been played away – the three men came off the green, put away their bowls, and turned down on to the canal bank towpath.

The valley became narrower and its sides steeper. Road, river and canal made their way as best they could, with only a twenty-yard strip of wasteland – a tangle of rank weeds, elderberry bushes and rubble, bleached debris of floods – separating river and canal. Along the far side of the river squeezed the road, rumbling from Monday to Saturday with swaying lorry-loads of cotton and wool and cloth. The valley wall on that side, draped with a network of stone-walled fields and precariously clinging farms and woods, came down sheer out of the sky into the backyards of a crouched stone row of weavers' cottages whose front doorsteps were almost part of the road. The river ran noisily over pebbles. On the strip of land between river and canal stood Top Wharf Pub – its buildings tucked in under the bank of the canal so that the towpath ran level with the back bedroom windows. On this side the valley wall, with overshadowing woods, dived straight into the black, motionless canal as if it must be a mile deep. The water was quite shallow, however, with its collapsed banks and accumulation of mud, so shallow that in some places the rushes grew right across. For years it had brought nothing to Top Wharf Pub but a black greasy damp and rats.

They turned down off the towpath into the wide, cobbled yard in front of the pub.

'You sit here. Now what would you like to drink?'

Michael sat on the cracked, weather-scrubbed bench in the yard under the bar-room window and asked for ginger beer.

'And see if he's come yet. And see if they have any rats ready.'

He had begun to notice the heat and now leaned back against the wall to get the last slice of shade under the eaves. But in no time the sun had moved out over the yard. The valley sides funnelled its rays down as into a trap, dazzling the quartz-points of the worn cobbles, burning the colour off everything. The flies were going wild, swirling in the air, darting and basking on the cobbles – big, green-glossed bluebottles that leapt on to his hand when he laid it along the hot bench.

In twos and threes men came over the hog-backed bridge leading from the road into the yard, or down off the towpath. Correct, leisurely and a little dazed from morning service, or in overalls that were torn and whitened from obscure Sabbath labours, all disappeared through the door. The hubbub inside thickened. Michael strained to catch some mention of Billy Red.

4

At last his father brought him his ginger beer and informed him that Billy Red had not arrived yet but everybody was expecting him and he shouldn't be long. They had some nice rats ready.

In spite of the heat, Michael suddenly did not feel like drinking. His whole body seemed to have become frailer and slightly faint, as with hunger. When he sipped, the liquid trickled with a cold, tasteless weight into his disinterested stomach.

He left the glass on the bench and went to the Gents. Afterwards he walked stealthily round the yard, looking in at the old stables and coach-house, the stony cave silences. Dust, cobwebs, rat droppings. Old timbers, old wheels, old harness. Barrels and rusty stoves. He listened for rats. Walking back across the blinding, humming yard he smelt roast beef and heard the clattering of the pub kitchen and saw through the open window fat arms working over a stove. The whole world was at routine Sunday dinner. The potatoes were already steaming, people sitting about killing time and getting impatient and wishing that something would fall out of the blue and knowing that nothing would. The idea stifled him, he didn't want to think of it. He went quickly back to the bench and sat down, his heart beating as if he had run.

A car nosed over the little bridge and stopped at the far side of the yard, evidently not sure whether it was permitted to enter the yard at all. Out of it stepped a well-to-do young man and a young woman. The young man unbuttoned his pale tweed jacket, thrust his hands into his trouser pockets and came sauntering towards the pub door, the girl on her high heels following beside him, patting her hair and looking round at the scenery as if she had just come up out of a dark pit. They stood at the door for a moment, improvising their final decisions about what she would drink, whether this was the right place, and whether she ought to come in. He was sure it was the right place, this was where they did it all right, and he motioned her to sit on the end of the bench beside Michael. Michael moved accommodatingly to the other end. She ignored him, however, and perched on the last ten inches of the bench, arrayed her wide-skirted, summery blue-flowered frock over her knees, and busied herself with her mirror. The flies whirled around, inspecting this new thing of scents.

Suddenly there came a shout from the doorway of the pub, long drawn words: 'Here comes the man.'

Immediately several crowded to the doorway, glasses in their hands.

'Here he comes.'

5

'The Red Killer!'

'Poor little beggar. He looks as if he lives on rat meat.'

'Draw him a half, Gab.'

Over the bridge and into the yard shambled a five-foot, ragged figure. Scarecrowish, tawny to colourless, exhausted, this was Billy Red, the rat-catcher. As a sideline he kept hens, and he had something of the raw, flea-bitten look of a red hen, with his small, sunken features and gingery hair. From the look of his clothes you would think he slept on the hen-house floor, under the roosts. One hand in his pocket, his back at a half-bend, he drifted aimlessly to a stop. Then, to show that after all he had only come for a sit in the sun, he sat down beside Michael with a long sigh.

'It's a grand day,' he announced. His voice was not strong – lungless, a shaky wisp, full of hen-fluff and dust.

Michael peered closely and secretly at this wrinkled, neglected fifty-year-old face shrunk on its small skull. Among the four-day stubble and enlarged pores and deep folds it was hard to make out anything, but there were one or two marks that might have been old rat bites. He had a little withered mouth and kept moving the lips about as if he couldn't get them comfortable. After a sigh he would pause a minute, leaning forward, one elbow on his knees, then sigh again, changing his position, the other elbow now on the other knee, like a man too weary to rest.

'Here you are, Billy.'

A hand held a half-pint high at the pub door like a sign and with startling readiness Billy leapt to his feet and disappeared into the pub, gathering the half-pint on the way and saying:

'I've done a daft bloody thing. I've come down all this way wi'out brass.'

There was an obliging roar of laughter and Michael found himself looking at the girl's powdered profile. She was staring down at her neatly-covered toe as it twisted this way and that, presenting all its polished surfaces.

Things began to sound livelier inside – sharp, loud remarks kicking up bursts of laughter and showering exclamations. The young man came out, composed, serious, and handed the girl a long-stemmed clear glass with a cherry in it. He sat down between her and Michael, splaying his knees as he did so and lunging his face forward to meet his streamingly raised pint – one smooth, expert motion.

'He's in there now,' he said, wiping his mouth. 'They're getting him ready.'

The girl gazed into his face, tilting her glass till the cherry bobbed against her pursed red lips, opening her eyes wide.

Michael looked past her to the doorway. A new figure had appeared. He supposed this must be the landlord, Gab – an aproned hemisphere and round, red greasy face that screwed itself up to survey the opposite hillside.

'Right,' called the landlord. 'I'll get 'em.' Away he went, wiping his hands on his apron, then letting them swing wide of his girth like penguin flippers, towards the coach-house. Now everybody came out of the pub and Michael stood up, surprised to see how many had been crowded in there. They were shouting and laughing, pausing to browse their pints, circulating into scattered groups. Michael went over and stood beside his father who was one of an agitated four. He had to ask twice before he could make himself heard. Even to himself his voice sounded thinner than usual, empty, as if at bottom it wanted nothing so much as to dive into his stomach and hide there in absolute silence, letting events go their own way.

'How many is he going to do?'

'I think they've got two.' His father half turned down towards him. 'It's usually two or three.'

Nobody took any notice of Billy Red who was standing a little apart, his hands hanging down from the slight stoop that seemed more or less permanent with him, smiling absently at the noisy, hearty groups. He brightened and straightened as the last man out of the pub came across, balancing a brimming pint glass. Michael watched. The moment the pint touched those shrivelled lips the pale little eye set with a sudden strangled intentness. His long, skinny, unshaven throat writhed and the beer shrank away in the glass. In two or three seconds he lowered the glass empty, wiped his mouth on his sleeve and looked around. Then as nobody stepped forward to offer him a fill-up he set the glass down to the cobbles and stood drying his hands on his jacket.

Michael's gaze shifted slightly, and he saw the girl. He recognised his own thoughts in her look of mesmerised incredulity. At her side the young man was watching too, but shrewdly, between steady drinks.

The sun seemed to have come to a stop directly above. Two or three men had taken their jackets off, with irrelevant, noisy clown-ing, a few sparring feints. Somebody suggested they all go and stand in the canal and Billy Red do his piece under water, and another laughed so hard at this that the beer came spurting from his nostrils. High up on the opposite slope Michael could see a line of

7

Sunday walkers, moving slowly across the dazed grey of the fields. Their coats would be over their shoulders, their ties in their pockets, their shoes agony, the girls asking to be pushed – but if they stood quite still they would feel a breeze. In the cobbled yard the heat had begun to dance.

'Here we are.'

The landlord waddled into the middle of the yard holding up an oblong wire cage. He set it down with a clash on the cobbles.

'Two of the best.'

Everybody crowded round. Michael squeezed to the front and crouched down beside the cage. There was a pause of admiration. Hunched in opposite corners of the cage, their heads low and drawn in and their backs pressed to the wires so that the glossy black-tipped hairs bristled out, were two big brown rats. They sat quiet. A long pinkish-grey tail, thick at the root as his thumb, coiled out by Michael's foot. He touched the hairy tip of it gently with his fore-finger.

'Watch out, lad!'

The rat snatched its tail in, leapt across the cage with a crash and gripping one of the zinc bars behind its curved yellow teeth, shook till the cage rattled. The other rat left its corner and began gliding to and fro along one side – a continuous low fluidity, sniffing up and down the bars. Then both rats stopped and sat up on their hind legs, like persons coming out of a trance, suddenly recognising people. Their noses quivered as they directed their set, grey-chinned, in-quisitive expressions at one face after another.

The landlord had been loosening the nooses in the end of two long pieces of dirty string. He lifted the cage again.

'Catch a tail, Walt.'

The group pressed closer. A hand came out and roamed in readi-ness under the high-held cage floor. The rats moved uneasily. The landlord gave the cage a shake and the rats crashed. A long tail swung down between the wires. The hand grabbed and pulled.

'Hold it.'

The landlord slipped the noose over the tail, down to the very butt, and pulled it tight. The caught rat, not quite convinced before but now understanding the whole situation, doubled round like a thing without bones, and bit and shook the bars and forced its nose out between them to get at the string that held its buttocks tight to the cage side.

'Just you hold that string, Walt. So's it can't get away when we open up.'

8

Now the landlord lifted the cage again, while Walt held his string tight. The other rat, watching the operation on its companion, had bunched up in a corner, sitting on its tail.

'Clever little beggar. You know what I'm after, don't you?'

The landlord gave the cage a shake, but the rat clung on, its pink feet gripping the wires of the cage floor like hands. He shook the cage violently.

'Move, you stubborn little beggar,' demanded the landlord. He went on shaking the cage with sharp, jerking movements.

Then the rat startled everybody. Squeezing still farther into its corner, it opened its mouth wide and began to scream – a harsh, ripping, wavering scream travelling out over the yard like some thin, metallic, dazzling substance that decomposed instantly. As one scream died the rat started another, its mouth wide. Michael had never thought a rat could make so much noise. As it went on at full intensity, his stomach began to twist and flex like a thick muscle. For a moment he was so worried by these sensations that he stopped looking at the rat. The landlord kept on shaking the cage and the scream shook in the air, but the rat clung on, still sitting on its tail.

'Give him a poke, Gab, stubborn little beggar!'

The landlord held the cage still, reached into his top pocket and produced a pencil. At this moment, Michael saw the girl, extricating herself from the press, pushing out backwards. The ring of rapt faces and still legs closed again. The rat was hurtling round the cage, still screaming, leaping over the other, attacking the wires first at this side then at that. All at once it crouched in a corner, silent. A hand came out and grabbed the loop of tail. The other noose was there ready. The landlord set the cage down.

Now the circle relaxed and everyone looked down at the two rats flattened on the cage bottom, their tails waving foolishly outside the wires.

'Well then, Billy,' said the landlord. 'How are they?'

Billy Red nodded and grinned.

'Them's grand,' he said. 'Grand.' His little rustling voice made Michael want to cough.

'Right. Stand back.'

Everybody backed obediently, leaving the cage, Walt with his foot on one taut string and the landlord with his foot on the other in the middle of an arena six or seven yards across. Michael saw the young man on the far side, his glass still half full in his hand. The girl was nowhere to be seen.

Billy Red peeled his coat off, exposing an old shirt, army issue,

9

most of the left arm missing. He pulled his trousers up under his belt, spat on his hands, and took up a position which placed the cage door a couple of paces or so from his left side and slightly in front of him. He bent forward a little more than usual, his arms hanging like a wary wrestler's, his eye fixed on the cage.

'Eye like a bloody sparrow-hawk,' somebody murmured.

There was a silence. The landlord waited, kneeling now beside the cage. Nothing disturbed the dramatic moment but the distant, brainless church bells.

'This one first, Walt,' said the landlord. 'Ready, Billy?'

He pushed down the lever that raised the cage door and let his rat have its full five- or six-yard length of string. He had the end looped round his hand. Walt kept his rat on a tight string.

Everybody watched intently. The freed rat pulled its tail in delicately and sniffed at the noose round it, ignoring the wide-open door. Then the landlord reached to tap the cage and in a flash the rat vanished.

Michael lost sight of it. But he saw Billy Red spin half-round and drop smack down on his hands and knees on the cobbles.

'He's got it!'

Billy Red's face was compressed in a snarl and as he snapped his head from side to side the dark, elongated body of the rat whipped around his neck. He had it by the shoulders. Michael's eyes fixed like cameras.

A dozen shakes, and Billy Red stopped, his head lowered. The rat hanging from his mouth was bunching and relaxing, bunching and relaxing. He waited. Everyone waited. Then the rat spasmed, fighting with all its paws, and Billy shook again wildly, the rat's tail flying like a lash. This time when he stopped the body hung down limply. The piece of string, still attached to the tail, trailed away across the cobbles.

Gently Billy took the rat from his mouth and laid it down. He stood up, spat a couple of times, and began to wipe his mouth, smiling shamefacedly. Everybody breathed out – an exclamation of marvelling disgust and admiration, and loud above the rest: 'Pint now, Billy?'

The landlord walked back into the pub and most of the audience followed him to refresh their glasses. Billy Red stood separate, still wiping his mouth with a scrap of snuff-coloured cloth.

Michael went over and bent to look at the dead rat. Its shoulders were wet-black with saliva, and the fur bitten. It lay on its left side, slightly curved, its feet folded, its eyes still round and bright in their alert, inquisitive expression. He touched its long, springy whiskers. A little drip of blood was puddling under its nose on the cobblestones. As he watched, a bluebottle alighted on its tail and sprang off again, then suddenly reappeared on its nose, inspecting the blood.

He walked over to the cage. Walt was standing there talking, his foot on the taut string. This rat crouched against the wires as if they afforded some protection. It made no sign of noticing Michael as he bent low over it. Its black beads stared outward fixedly, its hot brown flanks going in and out. There was a sparkle on its fur, and as he looked more closely, thinking it must be perspiration, he became aware of the heat again.

He stood up, a dull pain in his head. He put his hand to his scalp and pressed the scorch down into his skull, but that didn't seem to connect with the dull, thick pain.

'I'm off now, Dad,' he called.

'Already? Aren't you going to see this other one?'

'I think I'll go.' He set off across the yard.

'Finish your drink,' his father called after him.

He saw his glass almost full on the end of the white bench but walked past it and round the end of the pub and up on to the towpath. The sycamore trees across the canal arched over black damp shade and the still water. High up, the valley slopes were silvered now, frizzled with the noon brightness. The earthen towpath was like stone. Fifty yards along he passed the girl in the blue-flowered frock sauntering back towards the pub, pulling at the heads of the tall bank grasses.

'Have they finished yet?' she asked.

Michael shook his head. He found himself unable to speak. With all his strength he began to run.

Starting-points

1. *Talk about a time when you looked forward eagerly to an event (perhaps an 'entertainment' like Michael's) and then found it very different from what you had imagined. Look again at the events of the story and carefully note down how Michael's feelings develop and change.*
2. *Working in groups of five or six, prepare part of a radio programme called* Sport as Entertainment. *Each person plays the role of one of the*

11

story's characters; for example, the landlord, Billy Red, Michael, Michael's father, the girl in the blue-flowered frock. The interviewer (one of the group) questions each character about his or her thoughts and feelings during the events of the story. You will probably need to reread parts, or the whole of the story, and you may need to have a practice run-through. Tape-record the interviews and discuss your results.

3. Imagine you are a film director and prepare the scene in the pub yard for a filmed version. First, reread the section covering Billy Red's arrival to Michael's departure, jotting down some ideas for procedure. Then discuss your plan with one or two others and listen to their ideas. Now prepare a film script. As well as including all the necessary dialogue, your script could show camera positioning and techniques. (For example, close-ups on visual details that you think are important.) Where necessary, include notes on special effects and accompanying music. Finally, discuss the merits of some of the plans and their appropriateness to the story Sunday.

4. What are the different ways in which Billy Red and the girl would feel about what happened in the pub yard? Discuss how events seem different depending on whether you are involved in them or merely looking on with little possibility of affecting the course of action. Rewrite this part of the story from the point of view of either the girl in the blue-flowered frock or Billy Red.

Suggestions for Writing

A. Reread the story and list the details of description which contribute to its 'Sundayish' atmosphere. Then, in a style similar to that of Ted Hughes, write a description of your Saturday evening (or your Monday morning) to convey its atmosphere and your feelings about it.

B. Give an account of events up to the point when 'Everybody breathed out – an exclamation of marvelling disgust and admiration'. Does this describe the way you feel at this point in the story? Explain why you feel as you do.

GREAT UNCLE CROW

H. E. Bates

ONCE in the summertime, when the water-lilies were in bloom and the wheat was new in ear, his grandfather took him on a long walk up the river, to see his Uncle Crow. He had heard so much of Uncle Crow, so much that was wonderful and to be marvelled at, and for such a long time, that he knew him to be, even before that, the most remarkable fisherman in the world.

'Masterpiece of a man, your Uncle Crow,' his grandfather said. 'He could git a clothes-line any day and tie a brick on it and a mossel of cake and go out and catch a pike as long as your arm.'

When he asked what kind of cake his grandfather seemed irritated and said it was just like a boy to ask questions of that sort.

'Any kind o' cake,' he said. 'Plum cake. Does it matter? Carraway cake. Christmas cake if you like. Anything. I shouldn't wonder if he could catch a pretty fair pike with a cold baked tater.'

'Only a pike?'

'Times,' his grandfather said, 'I've seen him sittin' on the bank on a sweltering hot day like a furnace, when nobody was gettin' a bite not even off a bloodsucker. And there your Uncle Crow'd be a-pullin' 'em out by the dozen, like a man shellin' harvest beans.'

'And how does he come to be my Uncle Crow?' he said, 'if my mother hasn't got a brother? Nor my father.'

'Well,' his grandfather said, 'he's really your mother's own cousin, if everybody had their rights. But all on us call him Uncle Crow.'

'And where does he live?'

'You'll see,' his grandfather said. 'All by hisself. In a little titty bit of a house, by the river.'

The little titty bit of a house, when he first saw it, surprised him very much. It was not at all unlike a black tarred boat that had either slipped down a slope and stuck there on its way to launching or one that had been washed up and left there in a flood. The roof of brown tiles had a warp in it and the sides were mostly built, he thought, of tarred beer-barrels.

The two windows with their tiny panes were about as large as chess-boards and Uncle Crow had nailed underneath each of them a sill of sheet tin that was still a brilliant blue, each with the words 'Backache Pills' in white lettering on it, upside-down.

On all sides of the house grew tall feathered reeds. They enveloped it like gigantic whispering corn. Some distance beyond the great reeds the river went past in a broad slow arc, on magnificent kingly currents, full of long white islands of water-lilies, as big as china breakfast cups, shining and yellow-hearted in the sun.

He thought, on the whole, that that place, the river with the water-lilies, the little titty bit of a house, and the great forest of reeds talking between soft brown beards, was the nicest he had ever seen.

'Anybody about?' his grandfather called. 'Crow! – anybody at home?'

The door of the house was partly open, but at first there was no answer. His grandfather pushed open the door still farther with his foot. The reeds whispered down by the river and were answered, in the house, by a sound like the creek of bed springs.

'Who is't?'

'It's me, Crow,' his grandfather called. 'Lukey. Brought the boy over to have a look at you.'

A big gangling red-faced man with rusty hair came to the door. His trousers were black and very tight. His eyes were a smeary vivid blue, the same colour as the stripes of his shirt, and his trousers were kept up by a leather belt with brass escutcheons on it, like those on horses' harness.

'Thought very like you'd be out a-pikin',' his grandfather said.

'Too hot. How's Lukey boy? Ain't seed y' lately, Lukey boy.'

His lips were thick and very pink and wet, like cow's lips. He made a wonderful erupting jolly sound somewhat between a belch and a laugh.

'Comin' in it a minute?'

In the one room of the house was an iron bed with an old red check horse-rug spread over it and a stone copper in one corner and a bare wooden table with dirty plates and cups and a tin kettle on it. Two osier baskets and a scythe stood in another corner.

Uncle Crow stretched himself full length on the bed as if he was very tired. He put his knees in the air. His belly was tight as a bladder of lard in his black trousers, which were mossy green on the knees and seat.

'How's the fishin'?' his grandfather said. 'I bin tellin' the boy – '

Uncle Crow belched deeply. From where the sun struck full on

14

the tarred wall of the house there was a hot whiff of baking tar. But when Uncle Crow belched there was a smell like the smell of yeast in the air.

'It ain't bin all that much of a summer yit,' Uncle Crow said. 'Ain't had the rain.'

'Not like that summer you catched the big 'un down at Archer's Mill. I recollect you a-tellin' on me – '

'Too hot and dry by half,' Uncle Crow said. 'Gits in your gullet like chaff.'

'You recollect that summer?' his grandfather said. 'Nobody else a-fetching on 'em out only you – '

'Have a drop o' neck-oil,' Uncle Crow said.

The boy wondered what neck-oil was and presently, to his surprise, Uncle Crow and his grandfather were drinking it. It came out of a dark-green bottle and it was a clear bright amber, like cold tea, in the two glasses.

'The medder were yeller with 'em,' Uncle Crow said. 'Yeller as a guinea.'

He smacked his lips with a marvellously juicy, fruity sound. The boy's grandfather gazed at the neck-oil and said he thought it would be a corker if it was kept a year or two, but Uncle Crow said, 'Trouble is, Lukey boy, it's a terrible job to keep it. You start tastin' on it to see if it'll keep and then you taste on it again and you go on tastin' on it until they ain't a drop left as 'll keep.'

Uncle Crow laughed so much that the bed springs cackled underneath his bouncing trousers.

'Why is it called neck-oil?' the boy said.

'Boy,' Uncle Crow said, 'when you git older, when you git growed up, you know what'll happen to your gullet?'

'No.'

'It'll git sort o' rusted up inside. Like a old gutter pipe. So's you can't swaller very easy. Rusty as old Harry it'll git. You know that, boy?'

'No.'

'Well, it will. I'm tellin', on y'. And you know what y' got to do then?'

'No.'

'Every now and then you gotta git a drop o' neck-oil down it. So's to ease it. A drop o' neck-oil every once in a while – that's what you gotta do to keep the rust out.'

The boy was still contemplating the curious prospect of his neck rusting up inside in later years when Uncle Crow said, 'Boy, you go outside and jis' round the corner you'll see a bucket. You bring handful o' cresses out on it. I'll bet you're hungry, ain't you?'

'A little bit.'

He found the watercresses in the bucket, cool in the shadow of the little house, and when he got back inside with them Uncle Crow said, 'Now you put the cresses on that there plate there and then put your nose inside that there basin and see what's inside. What is't, eh?'

'Eggs.'

'Ought to be fourteen on 'em. Four-apiece and two over. What sort are they, boy?'

'Moorhens'.'

'You got a knowin' boy here, Lukey,' Uncle Crow said. He dropped the scaly red lid of one eye like an old cockerel going to sleep. He took another drop of neck-oil and gave another fruity, juicy laugh as he heaved his body from the bed. 'A very knowin' boy.'

Presently he was carving slices of thick brown bread with a great horn-handled shut-knife and pasting each slice with summery golden butter. Now and then he took another drink of neck-oil and once he said, 'You get the salt pot, boy, and empty a bit out on that there saucer, so's we can all dip in.'

Uncle Crow slapped the last slice of bread on to the buttered pile and then said, 'Boy, you take that there jug there and go a step or two up the path and dip yourself a drop o' spring water. You'll see it. It comes out of a little bit of a wall, jist by a doddle-willer.'

When the boy got back with the jug of spring water Uncle Crow was opening another bottle of neck-oil and his grandfather was saying, 'God a-mussy man, goo steady. You'll have me agoin' one way and another – '

'Man alive,' Uncle Crow said, 'and what's wrong with that?'

Then the watercress, the salt, the moorhens' eggs, the spring water, and the neck-oil were all ready. The moorhens' eggs were hard-boiled. Uncle Crow lay on the bed and cracked them with his teeth, just like big brown nuts, and said he thought the watercress was just about as nice and tender as a young lady.

'I'm sorry we ain't got the gold plate out though. I had it out a-Sunday.' He closed his old cockerel-lidded eye again and licked his tongue backwards and forwards across his lips and dipped another peeled egg in salt. 'You know what I had for my dinner a-Sunday, boy?'

'No.'

'A pussy-cat on a gold plate. Roasted with broad beans and new taters. Did you ever heerd talk of anybody eatin' a roasted pussy-cat, boy?'

'Yes.'

'You did?'

'Yes,' he said, 'that's a hare.'

'You got a very knowin' boy here, Lukey,' Uncle Crow said. 'A very knowin' boy.'

Then he screwed up a big dark-green bouquet of watercress and dipped it in salt until it was entirely frosted and then crammed it in one neat wholesale bite into his soft pink mouth.

'But not on a gold plate?' he said.

He had to admit that.

'No, not on a gold plate,' he said.

All that time he thought the fresh watercress, the moorhens' eggs, the brown bread and butter, and the spring water were the most delicious, wonderful things he had ever eaten in the world. He felt that only one thing was missing. It was that whenever his grandfather spoke of fishing Uncle Crow simply took another draught of neck-oil.

'When are you goin' to take us fishing?' he said.

'You et up that there egg,' Uncle Crow said. 'That's the last one. You et that there egg up and I'll tell you what.'

'What about gooin' as far as that big deep hole where the chub lay?' Grandfather said. 'Up by the back-brook – '

'I'll tell you what, boy,' Uncle Crow said, 'you git your grandfather to bring you over September time, of a morning, afore the steam's off the winders. Mushroomin' time. You come over and we'll have a bit o' bacon and mushroom for breakfast and then set into the pike. You see, boy, it ain't the pikin' season now. It's too hot. Too bright. It's too bright of afternoon, and they ain't a-bitin'.'

He took a long rich swig of neck-oil.

'Ain't that it, Lukey? That's the time, ain't it, mushroom time?'

'Thass it,' his grandfather said.

'Tot out,' Uncle Crow said. 'Drink up. My throat's jist easin' orf a bit.'

He gave another wonderful belching laugh and told the boy to be sure to finish up the last of the watercress and the bread and butter. The little room was rich with the smell of neck-oil, and the tarry sun-baked odour of the beer-barrels that formed its walls. And through the door came, always, the sound of reeds talking in their beards, and the scent of summer meadows drifting in from beyond

17

the great curl of the river with its kingly currents and its islands of full-blown lilies, white and yellow in the sun.

'I see the wheat's in ear,' his grandfather said. 'Ain't that the time for tench, when the wheat's in ear?'

'Mushroom time,' Uncle Crow said. 'That's the time. You git mushroom time here, and I'll fetch you a tench out as big as a cricket bat.'

He fixed the boy with an eye of wonderful, watery, glassy blue and licked his lips with a lazy tongue, and said, 'You know what colour a tench is, boy?'

'Yes,' he said.

'What colour?'

'The colour of the neck-oil.'

'Lukey,' Uncle Crow said, 'you got a very knowin' boy here. A very knowin' boy.'

After that, when there were no more cresses or moorhens' eggs, or bread and butter to eat, and his grandfather said he'd get hung if he touched another drop of neck-oil, he and his grandfather walked home across the meadows.

'What work does Uncle Crow do?' he said.

'Uncle Crow? Work? – well, he ain't – Uncle Crow? Well, he works, but he ain't what you'd call a reg'lar worker – '

All the way home he could hear the reeds talking in their beards. He could see the water-lilies that reminded him so much of the gold and white inside the moorhens' eggs. He could hear the happy sound of Uncle Crow laughing and sucking at the neck-oil, and crunching the fresh salty cresses into his mouth in the tarry little room.

He felt happy, too, and the sun was a gold plate in the sky.

Starting-points

1. *'He ain't what you'd call a reg'lar worker'. By this time in the story we know that Uncle Crow is more interested in relaxing, and in food and drink (especially drink!), than in any other activity – even fishing. But the writer has given us many clues earlier. Look for these in the description of Crow and his house and in what he says and does. See how many you can discover and make a list of them.*

2. *Working in threes, decide whether Crow, the boy and his grandfather all enjoyed the visit. Look through the story again and act it out concentrating on what each person is feeling, and what particular things give enjoyment and pleasure to each.*

3. *Imagine that an official from the local housing department arrives at Crow's house. His main responsibility is the welfare of old people and he has come to persuade Uncle Crow that he would be much better off in a new flat in town than in his makeshift house. Working in pairs, act out the interview between Crow and the official.*

4. *Work in pairs. Make a list of the ordinary and natural pleasures of summer life as experienced by the boy on his visit. Use the list as notes which the boy might use when interviewed for a radio programme called* The Simple Life. *Record the interview. Decide if there are any disadvantages in Crow's way of life.*

Suggestions for Writing

A. *Think of an old person (perhaps a relative or someone who lives near you) and write a story about a visit to their house. (Try to give the reader a clear impression of the kind of person from a description of the house as well as from the person's actions, and what he or she says.)*

B. *'The sun was a gold plate in the sky'. Write a poem or story about a day that you have particularly enjoyed.*

C. *Write a full description of Uncle Crow, starting with his physical characteristics and the way he lives, then analysing his character. (Refer to the story for your information and any notes you have made for Starting-point 1.)*

THROUGH
THE TUNNEL

Doris Lessing

GOING to the shore on the first morning of the holiday, the young English boy stopped at a turning of the path and looked down at a wild and rocky bay, and then over to the crowded beach he knew so well from other years. His mother walked on in front of him, carrying a bright-striped bag in one hand. Her other arm, swinging loose, was very white in the sun. The boy watched that white, naked arm, and turned his eyes, which had a frown behind them, towards the bay and back again to his mother. When she felt he was not with her, she swung round. 'Oh, there you are, Jerry!' she said. She looked impatient, then smiled. 'Why, darling, would you rather not come with me? Would you rather. . . .' She frowned, conscientiously worrying over what amusements he might secretly be longing for which she had been too busy or too careless to imagine. He was very familiar with that anxious, apologetic smile. Contrition sent him running after her. And yet, as he ran, he looked back over his shoulder at the wild bay; and all morning, as he played on the safe beach, he was thinking of it.

Next morning, when it was time for the routine of swimming and sunbathing, his mother said, 'Are you tired of the usual beach, Jerry? Would you like to go somewhere else?'

'Oh, no!' he said quickly, smiling at her out of that unfailing impulse of contrition – a sort of chivalry. Yet, walking down the path with her, he blurted out, 'I'd like to go and have a look at those rocks down there.'

She gave the idea her attention. It was a wild-looking place, and there was no one there, but she said, 'Of course, Jerry. When you've had enough, come to the big beach. Or just go straight back to the villa, if you like.' She walked away, that bare arm, now slightly reddened from yesterday's sun, swinging. And he almost ran after her again, feeling it unbearable that she should go by herself, but he did not.

She was thinking: Of course he's old enough to be safe without me. Have I been keeping him too close? He mustn't feel he ought to be with me. I must be careful.

He was an only child, eleven years old. She was a widow. She was determined to be neither possessive nor lacking in devotion. She went worrying off to her beach.

As for Jerry, once he saw that his mother had gained her beach, he began the steep descent to the bay. From where he was, high up among red-brown rocks, it was a scoop of moving bluish green fringed with white. As he went lower, he saw that it spread among small promontories and inlets of rough, sharp rock, and the crisping, lapping surface showed stains of purple and darker blue. Finally, as he ran sliding and scraping down the last few yards, he saw an edge of white surf, and the shallow, luminous movement of water over white sand, and, beyond that, a solid, heavy blue.

He ran straight into the water and began swimming. He was a good swimmer. He went out fast over the gleaming sand, over a middle region where rocks lay like discoloured monsters under the surface, and then he was in the real sea – a warm sea where irregular cold currents from the deep water shocked his limbs.

When he was so far out that he could look back not only on the little bay but past the promontory that was between it and the big beach, he floated on the buoyant surface and looked for his mother. There she was, a speck of yellow under an umbrella that looked like a slice of orange-peel. He swam back to shore, relieved at being sure she was there, but all at once very lonely.

On the edge of a small cape that marked the side of the bay away from the promontory was a loose scatter of rocks. Above them, some boys were stripping off their clothes. They came running, naked, down to the rocks. The English boy swam towards them, and kept his distance at a stone's throw. They were of that coast, all of them burned smooth dark brown, and speaking a language he did not understand. To be with them, of them, was a craving that filled his whole body. He swam a little closer; they turned and watched him with narrowed, alert dark eyes. Then one smiled and waved. It was enough. In a minute he had swum in and was on the rocks beside them, smiling with a desperate, nervous supplication. They shouted cheerful greetings at him, and then, as he preserved his nervous, uncomprehending smile, they understood that he was a foreigner strayed from his own beach, and they proceeded to forget him. But he was happy. He was with them.

They began diving again and again from a high point into a well of blue sea between rough, pointed rocks. After they had dived and come up, they swam round, hauled themselves up, and waited their turn to dive again. They were big boys – men to Jerry. He dived, and they watched him, and when he swam round to take his place, they made way for him. He felt he was accepted, and he dived again, carefully, proud of himself.

Soon the biggest of the boys poised himself, shot down into the water, and did not come up. The others stood about, watching. Jerry, after waiting for the sleek brown head to appear, let out a yell of warning; they looked at him idly and turned their eyes back towards the water. After a long time, the boy came up on the other side of a big dark rock, letting the air out of his lungs in a sputtering gasp and a shout of triumph. Immediately, the rest of them dived in. One moment the morning seemed full of chattering boys; the next, the air and the surface of the water were empty. But through the heavy blue, dark shapes could be seen moving and groping.

Jerry dived, shot past the school of underwater swimmers, saw a black wall of rock looming at him, touched it, and bobbed up at once to the surface, where the wall was a low barrier he could see across. There was no one visible; under him, in the water, the dim shapes of the swimmers had disappeared. Then one and then another of the boys came up on the far side of the barrier of rock, and he under-stood that they had swum through some gap or hole in it. He plunged down again. He could see nothing through the stinging salt water but the blank rock. When he came up, the boys were all on the diving rock, preparing to attempt the feat again. And now, in a panic of failure, he yelled up, in English, 'Look at me! Look!' and he began splashing and kicking in the water like a foolish dog.

They looked down gravely, frowning. He knew the frown. At moments of failure, when he clowned to claim his mother's atten-tion, it was with just this grave, embarrassed inspection that she rewarded him. Through his hot shame, feeling the pleading grin on his face like a scar that he could never remove, he looked up at the group of big brown boys on the rock and shouted '*Bonjour! Merci! Au revoir! Monsieur, monsieur!*' while he hooked his fingers round his ears and waggled them.

Water surged into his mouth; he choked, sank, came up. The rock, lately weighted with boys, seemed to rear up out of the water as their weight was removed. They were flying down past him, now, into the water; the air was full of falling bodies. Then the rock was empty in the hot sunlight. He counted one, two, three. . . .

At fifty he was terrified. They must all be drowning beneath him, in the watery caves of the rock! At a hundred he stared around him at the empty hillside, wondering if he should yell for help. He counted faster, faster, to hurry them up, to bring them to the surface quickly, to drown them quickly – anything rather than the terror of counting on and on into the blue emptiness of the morning. And then, at a hundred and sixty, the water beyond the rock was full of boys blowing like brown whales. They swam back to the shore without a look at him.

He climbed back to the diving rock and sat down, feeling the hot roughness of it under his thighs. The boys were gathering up their bits of clothing and running off along the shore to another promontory. They were leaving to get away from him. He cried openly, fists in his eyes. There was no one to see him, and he cried himself out.

It seemed to him that a long time had passed, and he swam out to where he could see his mother. Yes, she was still there, a yellow spot under an orange umbrella. He swam back to the big rock, climbed up, and dived into the blue pool among the fanged and angry boulders. Down he went, until he touched the wall of rock again. But the salt was so painful in his eyes that he could not see.

He came to the surface, swam to shore, and went back to the villa to wait for his mother. Soon she walked slowly up the path, swinging her striped bag, the flushed, naked arm dangling beside her. 'I want some swimming goggles,' he panted, defiant and beseeching.

She gave him a patient, inquisitive look as she said casually, 'Well of course, darling.'

But now, now, now! He must have them this minute, and no other time. He nagged and pestered until she went with him to a shop. As soon as she had bought the goggles, he grabbed them from her hand as if she were going to claim them for herself, and was off, running down the steep path to the bay.

Jerry swam out to the big barrier rock, adjusted the goggles, and dived. The impact of the water broke the rubber-enclosed vacuum, and the goggles came loose. He understood that he must swim down to the base of the rock from the surface of the water. He fixed the goggles tight and firm, filled his lungs, and floated, face down, on the water. Now he could see. It was as if he had eyes of a different kind – fish-eyes that showed everything clear and delicate and wavering in the bright water.

Under him, six or seven feet down, was a floor of perfectly clean, shining white sand, rippled firm and hard by the tides. Two greyish shapes steered there, like long, rounded pieces of wood or slate. They were fish. He saw them nose towards each other, poise motionless, make a dart forward, swerve off, and come round again. It was like a water dance. A few inches above them, the water sparkled as if sequins were dropping through it. Fish again – myriads of minute fish, the length of his finger-nail, were drifting through the water, and in a moment he could feel the innumerable tiny touches of them against his limbs. It was like swimming in flaked silver. The great rock the big boys had swum through rose sheer out of the white sand, black, tufted lightly with greenish weed. He could see no gap in it. He swam down to its base.

Again and again he rose, took a big chestful of air, and went down. Again and again he groped over the surface of the rock, feeling it, almost hugging it in the desperate need to find the entrance. And then, once, while he was clinging to the black wall, his knees came up and he shot his feet out forward and they met no obstacle. He had found the hole.

He gained the surface, clambered about the stones that littered the barrier rock until he found a big one, and, with this in his arms, let himself down over the side of the rock. He dropped, with the weight, straight to the sandy floor. Clinging tight to the anchor of stone, he lay on his side and looked in under the dark shelf at the place where his feet had gone. He could see the hole. It was an irregular, dark gap, but he could not see deep into it. He let go of his anchor, clung with his hands to the edges of the hole, and tried to push himself in.

He got his head in, found his shoulders jammed, moved them in sidewise, and was inside as far as his waist. He could see nothing ahead. Something soft and clammy touched his mouth, he saw a dark frond moving against the greyish rock, and panic filled him. He thought of octopuses, of clinging weed. He pushed himself out backward and caught a glimpse, as he retreated, of a harmless tentacle of seaweed drifting in the mouth of the tunnel. But it was enough. He reached the sunlight, swam to shore, and lay on the diving rock. He looked down in the blue well of water. He knew he must find his way through that cave, or hole, or tunnel, and out the other side.

First, he thought, he must learn to control his breathing. He let himself down into the water with another big stone in his arms, so that he could lie effortlessly on the bottom of the sea. He counted. One, two, three. He counted steadily. He could hear the movement of blood in his chest. Fifty-one, fifty-two. . . . His chest was hurting. He let go of the rock and went up into the air. He saw that the sun was low. He rushed to the villa and found his mother at her supper.

She said only 'Did you enjoy yourself?' and he said 'Yes'.

All night the boy dreamed of the water-filled cave in the rock, and as soon as breakfast was over he went to the bay.

That night his nose bled badly. For hours he had been under-water, learning to hold his breath, and now he felt weak and dizzy. His mother said, 'I shouldn't overdo things, darling, if I were you.'

That day and the next, Jerry exercised his lungs as if everything, the whole of his life, all that he would become, depended upon it. And again his nose bled at night, and his mother insisted on his coming with her the next day. It was a torment to him to waste a day of his careful self-training, but he stayed with her on that other beach, which now seemed a place for small children, a place where his mother might lie safe in the sun. It was not his beach.

He did not ask for permission, on the following day, to go to his beach. He went, before his mother could consider the complicated rights and wrongs of the matter. A day's rest, he discovered, had improved his count by ten. The big boys had made the passage while he counted a hundred and sixty. He had been counting fast, in his fright. Probably now, if he tried, he could get through that long tunnel, but he was not going to try yet. A curious, most unchildlike persistence, a controlled impatience, made him wait. In the mean-time, he lay underwater on the white sand, littered now by stones he had brought down from the upper air, and studied the entrance to the tunnel. He knew every jut and corner of it, as far as it was possible to see. It was as if he already felt its sharpness about his shoulders.

He sat by the clock in the villa, when his mother was not near, and checked his time. He was incredulous and then proud to find he could hold his breath without strain for two minutes. The words 'two minutes', authorised by the clock, brought the adventure that was so necessary to him close.

In another four days, his mother said casually one morning, they must go home. On the day before they left, he would do it. He would do it if it killed him, he said defiantly to himself. But two days before they were to leave – a day of triumph when he increased his count by fifteen – his nose bled so badly that he turned dizzy and had to lie limply over the big rock like a bit of seaweed, watching the thick red blood flow on to the rock and trickle slowly down to the sea. He was frightened. Supposing he turned dizzy in the tunnel? Supposing he died there, trapped? Supposing – his head went round, in the hot sun, and he almost gave up. He thought he would return to the house and lie down, and next summer, perhaps, when

25

he had another year's growth in him – *then* he would go through the hole.

But even after he had made the decision, or thought he had, he found himself sitting up on the rock and looking down into the water, and he knew that now, this moment, when his nose had only just stopped bleeding, when his head was still sore and throbbing – this was the moment when he would try. If he did not do it now, he never would. He was trembling with fear that he would not go, and he was trembling with horror at that long, long tunnel under the rock, under the sea. Even in the open sunlight the barrier rock seemed very wide and very heavy; tons of rock pressed down on where he would go. If he died there he would lie until one day – perhaps not before next year – those big boys would swim into it and find it blocked.

He put on his goggles, fitted them tight, tested the vacuum. His hands were shaking. Then he chose the biggest stone he could carry and slipped over the edge of the rock until half of him was in the cool, enclosing water and half in the hot sun. He looked up once at the empty sky, filled his lungs once, twice, and then sank fast to the bottom with the stone. He let it go and began to count. He took the edges of the hole in his hands and drew himself into it, wriggling his shoulders in sideways as he remembered he must, kicking himself along with his feet.

Soon he was clear inside. He was in a small rock-bound hole filled with yellowish-grey water. The water was pushing him up against the roof. The roof was sharp and pained his back. He pulled himself along with his hands – fast, fast – and used his legs as levers. His head knocked against something; a sharp pain dizzied him. Fifty, fifty-one, fifty-two. . . . He was without light, and the water seemed to press upon him with the weight of rock. Seventy-one, seventy-two. . . . There was no strain on his lungs. He felt like an inflated balloon, his lungs were so light and easy, but his head was pulsing.

He was being continually pressed against the sharp roof, which felt slimy as well as sharp. Again he thought of octopuses, and wondered if the tunnel might be filled with weed that could tangle him. He gave himself a panicky, convulsive kick forward, ducked his head, and swam. His feet and hands moved freely, as if in open water. The hole must have widened out. He thought he must be swimming fast, and he was frightened of banging his head if the tunnel narrowed.

A hundred, a hundred and one. . . . The water paled. Victory filled him. His lungs were beginning to hurt. A few more strokes and he

26

would be out. He was counting wildly; he said a hundred and fifteen, and then, a long time later, a hundred and fifteen again. The water was a clear jewel-green all around him. Then he saw, above his head, a crack running up through the rock. Sunlight was falling through it, showing the clean dark rock of the tunnel, a single mussel shell, and darkness ahead.

He was at the end of what he could do. He looked up at the crack as if it were filled with air and not water, as if he could put his mouth to it to draw in air. A hundred and fifteen, he heard himself say inside his head – but he had said that long ago. He must go on into the blackness ahead, or he would drown. His head was swelling, his lungs cracking. A hundred and fifteen, a hundred and fifteen pounded through his head, and he feebly clutched at rocks in the dark, pulling himself forward, leaving the brief space of sunlit water behind. He felt he was dying. He was no longer quite conscious. He struggled on in the darkness between lapses into unconsciousness. An immense, swelling pain filled his head, and then the darkness cracked with an explosion of green light. His hands, groping forward, met nothing, and his feet, kicking back, propelled him out into the open sea.

He drifted to the surface, his face turned up to the air. He was gasping like a fish. He felt he would sink now and drown; he could not swim the few feet back to the rock. Then he was clutching it and pulling himself up on to it. He lay face down, gasping. He could see nothing but a red-veined, clotted dark. His eyes must have burst, he thought; they were full of blood. He tore off his goggles and a gout of blood went into the sea. His nose was bleeding, and the blood had filled the goggles.

He scooped up handfuls of water from the cool, salty sea, to splash on his face, and did not know whether it was blood or salt water he tasted. After a time, his heart quieted, his eyes cleared, and he sat up. He could see the local boys, diving and playing half a mile away. He did not want them. He wanted nothing but to get back home and lie down.

In a short while, Jerry swam to shore and climbed slowly up the path to the villa. He flung himself on his bed and slept, waking at the sound of feet on the path outside. His mother was coming back. He rushed to the bathroom, thinking she must not see his face with blood-stains, or tear-stains, on it. He came out of the bathroom and met her as she walked into the villa, smiling, her eyes lighting up.

'Have a nice morning?' she asked, laying her hand on his warm brown shoulder a moment.

27

'Oh, yes, thank you,' he said.

'You look a bit pale.' And then, sharp and anxious, 'How did you bang your head?'

'Oh, just banged it,' he told her.

She looked at him closely. He was strained. His eyes were glazed looking. She was worried. And then she said to herself: Oh, don't fuss! Nothing can happen. He can swim like a fish.

They sat down to lunch together.

'Mummy,' he said, 'I can stay under water for two minutes – three minutes, at least.' It came bursting out of him.

'Can you darling?' she said. 'Well, I shouldn't overdo it. I don't think you ought to swim any more today.'

She was ready for a battle of wills, but he gave in at once. It was no longer of the least importance to go to the bay.

Starting-points

1. *Talk about Jerry's mother. What kind of person is she? Does she handle the situation (and Jerry) sensibly? Talk about a time when you knew of an adult who was similarly concerned about your actions and feelings.*

2. *Working in groups, talk about situations where you have tried to copy the actions of older people. Try out some of these incidents in drama. Decide whether these situations have always made you more mature.*

3. *Look again at the way the writer describes the safe beach and the wild bay, and note down some of the words she uses. Why are these descriptions important to the story?*

Suggestions for Writing

A. *Jerry clowned to get attention from the foreign boys. When they left he cried. But the next time he sees them he doesn't want them around. Describe briefly Jerry's behaviour and feelings on these occasions. What has happened to cause the change in his feelings?*

B. *Describe the careful preparations that Jerry made for his attempt on the tunnel. What does this episode reveal about his character?*

C. *Think of a time when you deliberately tackled something that (at the time) was terrifying, unknown or dangerous. Describe exactly how you set about it and what your feelings were.*

THE TROUT

Sean O'Faolain

ONE of the first places Julia always ran to when they arrived in
G—— was The Dark Walk. It is a laurel walk, very old; almost gone
wild; a lofty midnight tunnel of smooth, sinewy branches. Under-
foot the tough brown leaves are never dry enough to crackle: there is
always a suggestion of damp and cool trickle.

She raced right into it. For the first few yards she always had the
memory of the sun behind her, then she felt the dusk closing swiftly
down on her so that she screamed with pleasure and raced on to
reach the light at the far end; and it was always just a little too long in
coming so that she emerged gasping, clasping her hands, laughing,
drinking in the sun. When she was filled with the heat and glare she
would turn and consider the ordeal again.

This year she had the extra joy of showing it to her small brother,
and of terrifying him as well as herself. And for him the fear lasted
longer because his legs were so short and she had gone out at the far
end while he was still screaming and racing.

When they had done this many times they came back to the house
to tell everybody that they had done it. He boasted. She mocked.
They squabbled.

'Cry babby!'

'You were afraid yourself, so there!'

'I won't take you any more.'

'You're a big pig.'

'I hate you.'

Tears were threatening, so somebody said, 'Did you see the well?'
She opened her eyes at that and held up her long lovely neck
suspiciously and decided to be incredulous. She was twelve and at
that age little girls are beginning to suspect most stories: they have
already found out too many, from Santa Claus to the stork. How
could there be a well! In The Dark Walk? That she had visited year
after year? Haughtily she said, 'Nonsense.'

But she went back, pretending to be going somewhere else, and

30

she found a hole scooped in the rock at the side of the walk, choked with damp leaves, so shrouded by ferns that she uncovered it only after much searching. At the back of this little cavern there was about a quart of water. In the water she suddenly perceived a panting trout. She rushed for Stephen and dragged him to see, and they were both so excited that they were no longer afraid of the darkness as they hunched down and peered in at the fish panting in his tiny prison, his silver stomach going up and down like an engine.

Nobody knew how the trout got there. Even old Martin in the kitchen garden laughed and refused to believe that it was there, or pretended not to believe, until she forced him to come down and see. Kneeling and pushing back his tattered old cap, he peered in.

'Be cripes, you're right. How the divil in hell did that fella get there?'

She stared at him suspiciously.

'You knew?' she accused; but he said, 'The divil a' know,' and reached down to lift it out. Convinced, she hauled him back. If she had found it, then it was her trout.

Her mother suggested that a bird had carried the spawn. Her father thought that in the winter a small streamlet might have carried it down there as a baby, and it had been safe until the summer came and the water began to dry up. She said, 'I see,' and went back to look again and consider the matter in private. Her brother remained behind, wanting to hear the whole story of the trout, not really interested in the actual trout but much interested in the story which his mummy began to make up for him on the lines of, 'So one day Daddy Trout and Mummy Trout. . . .' When he retailed it to her she said 'Pooh'.

It troubled her that the trout was always in the same position; he had no room to turn. All the time the silver belly went up and down; otherwise he was motionless. She wondered what he ate, and in between visits to Joey Pony and the boat, and a bathe to get cool, she thought of his hunger. She brought him down bits of dough; once she brought him a worm. He ignored the food. He just went on panting. Hunched over him she thought how all the winter, while she was at school, he had been in there. All the winter, in The Dark Walk, all day, all night, floating around alone. She drew the leaf of her hat down around her ears and chin and stared. She was still thinking of it as she lay in bed.

It was late June, the longest days of the year. The sun had sat still for a week, burning up the world. Although it was after ten o'clock it

31

was still bright and still hot. She lay on her back under a single sheet, with her long legs spread, trying to keep cool. She could see the D of the moon through the fir tree – they slept on the ground floor. Before they went to bed her mummy had told Stephen the story of the trout again, and she, in her bed, had resolutely presented her back to them and read her book. But she had kept one ear cocked.

'And so, in the end, this naughty fish who would not stay at home got bigger and bigger and bigger, and the water got smaller and smaller. . . .'

Passionately she had whirled and cried, 'Mummy, don't make it a horrible old moral story!' Her mummy had brought in a fairy godmother then, who sent lots of rain, and filled the well, and a stream poured out and the trout floated away down to the river below. Staring at the moon she knew that there are no such things as fairy godmothers and that the trout, down in The Dark Walk, was panting like an engine. She heard somebody unwind a fishing-reel. Would the *beasts* fish him out!

She sat up. Stephen was a hot lump of sleep, lazy thing. The Dark Walk would be full of little scraps of moon. She leaped up and looked out the window, and somehow it was not so lightsome now that she saw the dim mountains far away and the black firs against the breathing land and heard a dog say *bark-bark*. Quietly she lifted the ewer of water and climbed out the window and scuttled along the cool but cruel gravel down to the maw of the tunnel. Her pyjamas were very short so that when she splashed water it wet her ankles. She peered into the tunnel. Something alive rustled inside there. She raced in and up and down she raced, and flurried, and cried aloud, 'Oh, gosh, I can't find it,' and then at last she did. Kneeling down in the damp, she put her hand into the slimy hole. When the body lashed they were both mad with fright. But she gripped him and shoved him into the ewer and raced, with her teeth ground, out to the other end of the tunnel and down the steep paths to the river's edge.

All the time she could feel him lashing his tail against the side of the ewer. She was afraid he would jump right out. The gravel cut into her soles until she came to the cool ooze of the river's bank where the moon mice on the water crept into her feet. She poured out, watching until he plopped. For a second he was visible in the water. She hoped he was not dizzy. Then all she saw was the glimmer of the moon in the silent-flowing river, the dark firs, the dim mountains, and the radiant pointed face laughing down at her out of the empty sky.

She scuttled up the hill, in the window, plonked down the ewer, and flew through the air like a bird into bed. The dog said *bark-bark*. She heard the fishing-reel whirring. She hugged herself and giggled. Like a river of joy her holiday spread before her.

In the morning Stephen rushed to her, shouting that 'he' was gone, and asking 'where' and 'how'. Lifting her nose in the air she said superciliously, 'Fairy godmother, I suppose?' and strolled away patting the palms of her hands.

Starting-points

1. *Find in the story a number of examples of the situation of being trapped. Look particularly at the dark alley, the trout in its hole, Julia in bed obliged to overhear a story she rejects, and the trout in the ewer. Jot down words and phrases which indicate being shut in, terror and struggle.*

   Talk about your own reactions to being in dark, enclosed situations. You may perhaps have memories of being trapped in a dark room or cupboard as a child or have had dreams of being shut in. Discuss the feelings that go with this type of situation. Can you suggest any reasons for this kind of fear, which is common to us all?

2. *Working in pairs, decide whether Julia is putting any of her own feelings into the situation of the fish. When she deliberately frees it, does this action show something about what she is claiming for herself?*

3. *Talk about the stories which are told by adults to children. Discuss stories which were told to you and any sensations of betrayal you experienced when you found you could no longer believe them.*

Suggestions for Writing

A. *Retell the story's events as they would be seen by Julia's mother.*

B. *Write out, in the form of a script for a play, the conversation that might have taken place between the parents and the two children. (Think particularly what questions each child would have asked and how the parents would have answered them. Make sure that you show the parents' explanations differ according to which child they are speaking to.)*

C. *Is it true, do you think, that we become gradually more capable of coping sympathetically with the real world without requiring the interpretations that other people give? How do Julia and her brother represent different stages in development? How is Julia's relationship with adults different from Stephen's?*

THE PARSLEY GARDEN

William Saroyan

ONE day in August Al Condraj was wandering through Woolworth's without a penny to spend when he saw a small hammer that
was not a toy but a real hammer, and he was possessed with a
longing to have it. He believed it was just what he needed by which
to break the monotony and with which to make something. He had
gathered some first-class nails from Foley's Packing House where
the boxmakers worked and where they had carelessly dropped at
least fifteen cents' worth. He had gladly gone to the trouble of
gathering them together because it had seemed to him that a nail, as
such, was not something to be wasted. He had the nails, perhaps a
half pound of them, at least two hundred of them, in a paper bag in
the apple box in which he kept his junk at home.

Now, with the ten-cent hammer he believed he could make something out of box wood and the nails, although he had no idea what.
Some sort of a table perhaps, or a small bench.

At any rate he took the hammer and slipped it into the pocket of
his overalls, but just as he did so a man took him firmly by the arm
without a word and pushed him to the back of the store into a small
office. Another man, an older one, was seated behind a desk in the
office, working with papers. The younger man, the one who had
captured him, was excited and his forehead was covered with
sweat.

'Well,' he said, 'here's one more of them.'

The man behind the desk got to his feet and looked Al Condraj up
and down.

'What's *he* swiped?'

'A hammer.' The young man looked at Al with hatred. 'Hand it
over,' he said.

The boy brought the hammer out of his pocket and handed it to
the young man, who said, 'I ought to hit you over the head with it,
that's what I ought to do.'

35

He turned to the older man, the boss, the manager of the store, and he said, 'What do you want me to do with him?'

'Leave him with me,' the older man said.

The younger man stepped out of the office, and the older man sat down and went back to work. Al Condraj stood in the office fifteen minutes before the older man looked at him again.

'Well,' he said.

Al didn't know what to say. The man wasn't looking at him, he was looking at the door.

Finally Al said, 'I didn't mean to steal it. I just need it and I haven't got any money.'

'Just because you haven't got any money doesn't mean you've got a right to steal things,' the man said. 'Now, does it?'

'No, sir.'

'Well, what am I going to do with you? Turn you over to the police?'

Al didn't say anything, but he certainly didn't want to be turned over to the police. He hated the man, but at the same time he realised somebody else could be a lot tougher than he was being.

'If I let you go, will you promise never to steal from this store again?'

'Yes, sir.'

'All right,' the man said. 'Go out this way and don't come back to this store until you've got some money to spend.'

He opened a door to the hall that led to the alley, and Al Condraj hurried down the hall and out into the alley.

The first thing he did when he was free was laugh, but he knew he had been humiliated and he was deeply ashamed. It was not in his nature to take things that did not belong to him. He hated the young man who had caught him and he hated the manager of the store who had made him stand in silence in the office so long. He hadn't liked it at all when the young man had said he ought to hit him over the head with the hammer.

He should have had the courage to look him straight in the eye and say, 'You and who else?'

Of course he *had* stolen the hammer and he had been caught, but it seemed to him he oughtn't to have been so humiliated.

After he had walked three blocks he decided he didn't want to go home just yet, so he turned around and started walking back to town. He almost believed he meant to go back and say something to the young man who had caught him. And then he wasn't sure he didn't mean to go back and steal the hammer again, and this time *not* get caught. As long as he had been made to feel like a thief anyway, the least he ought to get out of it was the hammer.

Outside the store he lost his nerve, though. He stood in the street, looking in, for at least ten minutes.

Then, crushed and confused and now bitterly ashamed of himself, first for having stolen something, then for having been caught, then for having been humiliated, then for not having guts enough to go back and do the job right, he began walking home again, his mind so troubled that he didn't greet his pal Pete Wawchek when they came face to face outside Graf's Hardware.

When he got home he was too ashamed to go inside and examine his junk, so he had a long drink of water from the faucet in the back yard. The faucet was used by his mother to water the stuff she planted every year: okra, bell peppers, tomatoes, cucumbers, onions, garlic, mint, egg-plants and parsley.

His mother called the whole business the parsley garden, and every night in the summer she would bring chairs out of the house and put them around the table she had had Ondro, the neighbourhood handyman, make for her for fifteen cents, and she would sit at the table and enjoy the cool of the garden and the smell of the things she had planted and tended.

Sometimes she would even make a salad and moisten the flat old-country bread and slice some white cheese, and she and he would have supper in the parsley garden. After supper she would attach the water hose to the faucet and water her plants and the place would be cooler than ever and it would smell real good, real fresh and cool and green, all the different growing things making a green-garden smell out of themselves and the air and the water.

After the long drink of water he sat down where the parsley itself was growing and he pulled a handful of it out and slowly ate it. Then he went inside and told his mother what had happened. He even told her what he had *thought* of doing after he had been turned loose: to go back and steal the hammer again.

'I don't want you to steal,' his mother said in broken English. 'Here is ten cents. You go back to that man and you give him this money and you bring it home, that hammer.'

'No,' Al Condraj said. 'I won't take your money for something I don't really need. I just thought I ought to have a hammer, so I could make something if I felt like it. I've got a lot of nails and some box wood, but I haven't a hammer.'

'Go buy it, that hammer,' his mother said.

'No,' Al said.

37

'All right,' his mother said. 'Shut up.'

That's what she always said when she didn't know what else to say.

Al went out and sat on the steps. His humiliation was beginning to really hurt now. He decided to wander off along the railroad tracks to Foley's because he needed to think about it some more. At Foley's he watched Johnny Gale nailing boxes for ten minutes, but Johnny was too busy to notice him or talk to him, although one day at Sunday school, two or three years ago, Johnny had greeted him and said, 'How's the boy?' Johnny worked with a boxmaker's hatchet and everybody in Fresno said he was the fastest boxmaker in town. He was the closest thing to a machine any packing house ever saw. Foley himself was proud of Johnny Gale.

Al Condraj finally set out for home because he didn't want to get in the way. He didn't want somebody working hard to notice that he was being watched and maybe say to him, 'Go on, beat it.' He didn't want Johnny Gale to do something like that. He didn't want to invite another humiliation.

On the way home he looked for money but all he found was the usual pieces of broken glass and rusty nails, the things that were always cutting his bare feet every summer.

When he got home his mother had made a salad and set the table, so he sat down to eat, but when he put the food in his mouth he just didn't care for it. He got up and went into the three-room house and got his apple box out of the corner of his room and went through his junk. It was all there, the same as yesterday.

He wandered off back to town and stood in front of the closed store, hating the young man who had caught him, and then he went along to the Hippodrome and looked at the display photographs from the two movies that were being shown that day.

Then he went along to the public library to have a look at all the books again, but he didn't like any of them, so he wandered around town some more, and then around half-past eight he went home and went to bed.

His mother had already gone to bed because she had to be up at five to go to work at Inderneden's, packing figs. Some days there would be work all day, some days there would be only half a day of it, but whatever his mother earned during the summer had to keep them the whole year.

He didn't sleep much that night because he couldn't get over what had happened, and he went over six or seven ways by which to adjust the matter. He went so far as to believe it would be necessary to kill the young man who had caught him. He also believed it would be necessary for him to steal systematically and successfully the rest of his life. It was a hot night and he couldn't sleep.

Finally, his mother got up and walked barefooted to the kitchen for a drink of water and on the way back she said to him softly, 'Shut up.'

When she got up at five in the morning he was out of the house, but that had happened many times before. He was a restless boy, and he kept moving all the time every summer. He was making mistakes and paying for them, and he had just tried stealing and had been caught at it and he was troubled. She fixed her breakfast, packed her lunch and hurried off to work, hoping it would be a full day.

It was a full day, and then there was overtime, and although she had no more lunch she decided to work on for the extra money, anyway. Almost all the other packers were staying on, too, and her neighbour across the alley, Leeza Ahboot, who worked beside her, said, 'Let us work until the work stops, then we'll go home and fix a supper between us and eat it in your parsley garden where it's so cool. It's a hot day and there's no sense not making an extra fifty or sixty cents.'

When the two women reached the garden it was almost nine o'clock, but still daylight, and she saw her son nailing pieces of box wood together, making something with a hammer. It looked like a bench. He had already watered the garden and tidied up the rest of the yard, and the place seemed very nice, and her son seemed very serious and busy. She and Leeza went straight to work for their supper, picking bell peppers and tomatoes and cucumbers and a great deal of parsley for the salad.

Then Leeza went to her house for some bread which she had baked the night before, and some white cheese, and in a few minutes they were having supper together and talking pleasantly about the successful day they had had. After supper, they made Turkish coffee over an open fire in the yard. They drank the coffee and smoked a cigarette apiece, and told one another stories about their experiences in the old country and here in Fresno, and then they looked into their cups at the grounds to see if any good fortune was indicated, and there was: health and work and supper out of doors in the summer, and enough money for the rest of the year.

Al Condraj worked and overheard some of the things they said, and then Leeza went home to go to bed, and his mother said, 'Where you get it, that hammer, Al?'

'I got it at the store.'

'How you get it? You steal it?'

Al Condraj finished the bench and sat on it. 'No,' he said. 'I didn't steal it.'

'How you get it?'

'I worked at the store for it,' Al said.

'The store where you steal it yesterday?'

'Yes.'

'Who give you job?'

'The boss.'

'What you do?'

'I carried different stuff to the different counters.'

'Well, that's good,' the woman said. 'How long you work for that little hammer?'

'I worked all day,' Al said. 'Mr Clemmer gave me the hammer after I'd worked one hour, but I went right on working. The fellow who caught me yesterday showed me what to do, and we worked together. We didn't talk, but at the end of the day he took me to Mr Clemmer's office and he told Mr Clemmer that I'd worked hard all day and ought to be paid at least a dollar.'

'That's good,' the woman said.

'So Mr Clemmer put a silver dollar on his desk for me, and then the fellow who caught me yesterday told him the store needed a boy like me every day, for a dollar a day, and Mr Clemmer said I could have the job.'

'That's good,' the woman said. 'You can make a little money for yourself.'

'I left the dollar on Mr Clemmer's desk,' Al Condraj said, 'and I told them both I didn't want the job.'

'Why you say that?' the woman said. 'Dollar a day for eleven-year-old boy good money. Why you not take job?'

'Because I hate the both of them,' the boy said. 'I would never work for people like that. I just looked at them and picked up my hammer and walked out. I came home and I made this bench.'

'All right,' his mother said. 'Shut up.'

His mother went inside and went to bed, but Al Condraj sat on the bench he had made and smelled the parsley garden and didn't feel humiliated any more.

But nothing could stop him from hating the two men, even though he knew they hadn't done anything they shouldn't have done.

Starting-points

1. *Talk with others and try to find full and satisfactory answers to the following questions: What were Al's reasons for stealing the hammer? Why does he feel so humiliated afterwards? How does he cope with his humiliation? Is he right to refuse the job? (You will find it helpful to look through the story again and perhaps also to draw on your experiences of similar situations.)*

2. *Act out the situation in the store when Al is caught stealing and taken to Mr Clemmer's office by the younger man. Then act out the situation between the same three people later in the story when Al refuses the money. In what ways have the attitudes and feelings of the three changed?*

3. *Talk about whether Mr Clemmer dealt effectively with Al. What measures would you use to deal with shop-lifting?*
   Talk about whether it is possible to feel hatred for someone, knowing at the same time that they don't deserve to be hated.

4. *An English-speaking foreign visitor has been caught shop-lifting at a branch of Woolworth's in this country. Working in pairs, talk about how he or she felt and what the reasons for stealing were. Write out the conversation between the store manager and the visitor. Try this out and perhaps record it.*

Suggestions for Writing

A. *Retell the events of the story as they would be seen by the young man who first caught Al stealing the hammer.*

B. *Note down the words and phrases the writer uses to describe the parsley garden at Al's house. Why is the garden important to Al and his mother? Use your evidence and ideas to write an explanation in a letter of reply from the author of the story to a reader who has written complaining that a better title would be* The Hammer.

ARABY

James Joyce

NORTH RICHMOND STREET, being blind, was a quiet street except at the hour when the Christian Brothers' School set the boys free. An uninhabited house of two storeys stood at the blind end, detached from its neighbours in a square ground. The other houses of the street, conscious of decent lives within them, gazed at one another with brown imperturbable faces.

The former tenant of our house, a priest, had died in the back drawing-room. Air, musty from having been long enclosed, hung in all the rooms, and the waste room behind the kitchen was littered with old useless papers. Among these I found a few paper-covered books, the pages of which were curled and damp: *The Abbot*, by Walter Scott, *The Devout Communicant* and *The Memoirs of Vidocq*. I like the last best because its leaves were yellow. The wild garden behind the house contained a central apple tree and a few straggling bushes, under one of which I found the late tenant's rusty bicycle-pump. He had been a very charitable priest; in his will he had left all his money to institutions and the furniture of his house to his sister.

When the short days of winter came, dusk fell before we had well eaten our dinners. When we met in the street the houses had grown sombre. The space of sky above us was the colour of ever-changing violet and towards it the lamps of the street lifted their feeble lanterns. The cold air stung us and we played till our bodies glowed. Our shouts echoed in the silent street. The career of our play brought us through the dark muddy lanes behind the houses, where we ran the gauntlet of the rough tribes from the cottages, to the back doors of the dark dripping gardens where odours arose from the ashpits, to the dark odorous stables where a coachman smoothed and combed the horse or shook music from the buckled harness. When we returned to the street, light from the kitchen windows had filled the areas. If my uncle was seen turning the corner, we hid in the shadow until we had seen him safely housed. Or if Mangan's sister came out on the doorstep to call her brother in to his tea, we watched her from our shadow peer up and down the street. We waited to see whether she would remain or go in and, if she remained, we left our shadow and walked up to Mangan's steps resignedly. She was waiting for us, her figure defined by the light from the half-opened door. Her brother always teased her before he obeyed, and I stood by the railings looking at her. Her dress swung as she moved her body, and the soft rope of her hair tossed from side to side.

Every morning I lay on the floor in the front parlour watching her door. The blind was pulled down to within an inch of the sash so that I could not be seen. When she came out on the doorstep my heart leaped. I ran to the hall, seized my books, and followed her. I kept her brown figure always in my eye and, when we came near the point at which our ways diverged, I quickened my pace and passed her. This happened morning after morning. I had never spoken to her except for a few casual words, and yet her name was like a summons to all my foolish blood.

Her image accompanied me even in places the most hostile to romance. On Saturday evenings when my aunt went marketing I had to go to carry some of the parcels. We walked through the flaring streets, jostled by drunken men and bargaining women, amid the curses of labourers, the shrill litanies of shop-boys who stood on guard by the barrels of pigs' cheeks, the nasal chanting of street-singers, who sang a *come-all-you* about O'Donovan Rossa, or a ballad about the troubles in our native land. These noises converged in a single sensation of life for me: I imagined that I bore my chalice safely through a throng of foes. Her name sprang to my lips at moments in strange prayers and praises which I myself did not understand. My eyes were often full of tears (I could not tell why) and at times a flood from my heart seemed to pour itself out into my bosom. I thought little of the future. I did not know whether I would ever speak to her or not or, if I spoke to her, how I could tell her of my confused adoration. But my body was like a harp and her words and gestures were like fingers running upon the wires.

One evening I went into the back drawing-room in which the priest had died. It was a dark rainy evening and there was no sound in the house. Through one of the broken panes I heard the rain impinge upon the earth, the fine incessant needles of water playing in the sodden beds. Some distant lamp or lighted window gleamed below me. I was thankful that I could see so little. All my senses seemed to desire to veil themselves and, feeling that I was about to slip from them, I pressed the palms of my hands together until they trembled, murmuring 'O love! O love!' many times.

At last she spoke to me. When she addressed the first words to me I was so confused that I did not know what to answer. She asked me was I going to *Araby*. I forgot whether I answered yes or no. It would be a splendid bazaar; she said she would love to go.

'And why can't you?' I asked.

While she spoke she turned a silver bracelet round and round her wrist. She could not go, she said, because there would be a retreat that week in her convent. Her brother and two other boys were fighting for their caps, and I was alone at the railings. She held one of the spikes, bowing her head towards me. The light from the lamp opposite our door caught the white curve of her neck, lit up her hair that rested there and, falling, lit up the hand upon the railing. It fell over one side of her dress and caught the white border of a petticoat, just visible as she stood at ease.

'It's well for you,' she said.

'If I go,' I said, 'I will bring you something.'

What innumerable follies laid waste my waking and sleeping thoughts after that evening! I wished to annihilate the tedious intervening days. I chafed against the work of school. At night in my bedroom and by day in the class-room her image came between me and the page I strove to read. The syllables of the word *Araby* were called to me through the silence in which my soul luxuriated and cast an Eastern enchantment over me. I asked for leave to go to the bazaar on Saturday night. My aunt was surprised, and hoped it was not some Freemason affair. I answered few questions in class. I watched my master's face pass from amiability to sternness; he hoped I was not beginning to idle. I could not call my wandering thoughts together. I had hardly any patience with the serious work of life which, now that it stood between me and my desire, seemed to me child's play, ugly monotonous child's play.

On Saturday morning I reminded my uncle that I wished to go to the bazaar in the evening. He was fussing at the hall-stand, looking for the hat-brush, and answered me curtly, 'Yes, boy, I know.'

As he was in the hall I could not go into the front parlour and lie at the window. I felt the house in bad humour and walked slowly towards the school. The air was pitilessly raw and already my heart misgave me.

When I came home to dinner my uncle had not yet been home. Still it was early. I sat staring at the clock for some time and, when its ticking began to irritate me, I left the room. I mounted the staircase and gained the upper part of the house. The high, cold, empty, gloomy rooms liberated me and I went from room to room singing.

From the front window I saw my companions playing below in the street. Their cries reached me weakened and indistinct and, leaning my forehead against the cool glass, I looked over at the dark house where she lived. I may have stood there for an hour, seeing nothing but the brown-clad figure cast by my imagination, touched discreetly by the lamplight at the curved neck, at the hand upon the railings and at the border below the dress.

When I came downstairs again I found Mrs Mercer sitting at the fire. She was an old, garrulous woman, a pawnbroker's widow, who collected used stamps for some pious purpose. I had to endure the gossip of the tea-table. The meal was prolonged beyond an hour and still my uncle did not come. Mrs Mercer stood up to go: she was sorry she couldn't wait any longer, but it was after eight o'clock and she did not like to be out late, as the night air was bad for her.

When she had gone I began to walk up and down the room, clenching my fists. My aunt said, 'I'm afraid you may put off your bazaar for this night of Our Lord.'

At nine o'clock I heard my uncle's latchkey in the hall door. I heard him talking to himself and heard the hall-stand rocking when it had received the weight of his overcoat. I could interpret these signs. When he was midway through his dinner I asked him to give me the money to go to the bazaar. He had forgotten.

'The people are in bed and after their first sleep now,' he said.

I did not smile. My aunt said to him energetically, 'Can't you give him the money and let him go? You've kept him late enough as it is.'

My uncle said he was very sorry he had forgotten. He said he believed in the old saying 'All work and no play makes Jack a dull boy'. He asked me where I was going and, when I had told him a second time, he asked me did I know *The Arab's Farewell to His Steed*. When I left the kitchen he was about to recite the opening lines of the piece to my aunt.

I held a florin tightly in my hand as I strode down Buckingham Street towards the station. The sight of the streets thronged with buyers and glaring with gas recalled to me the purpose of my journey. I took my seat in a third-class carriage of a deserted train. After an intolerable delay the train moved out of the station slowly. It crept onward among ruinous houses and over the twinkling river. At Westland Row Station a crowd of people pressed to the carriage doors; but the porters moved them back, saying that it was a special train for the bazaar. I remained alone in the bare carriage. In a few minutes the train drew up beside an improvised wooden platform. I passed out on to the road and saw by the lighted dial of a clock that it

45

was ten minutes to ten. In front of me was a large building which displayed the magical name.

I could not find any sixpenny entrance and, fearing that the bazaar would be closed, I passed in quickly through a turnstile, handing a shilling to a weary-looking man. I found myself in a big hall girded at half its height by a gallery. Nearly all the stalls were closed and the greater part of the hall was in darkness. I recognised a silence like that which pervades a church after a service. I walked into the centre of the bazaar timidly. A few people were gathered about the stalls which were still open. Before a curtain, over which the words *Café Chantant* were written in coloured lamps, two men were counting money on a salver. I listened to the fall of the coins.

Remembering with difficulty why I had come, I went over to one of the stalls and examined porcelain vases and flowered tea-sets. At the door of the stall a young lady was talking and laughing with two young gentlemen. I remarked their English accents and listened vaguely to their conversation.

'Oh, I never said such a thing!'

'Oh, but you did!'

'Oh, but I didn't!'

'Didn't she say that?'

'Yes. I heard her.'

'Oh, there's a . . . fib!'

Observing me, the young lady came over and asked me did I wish to buy anything. The tone of her voice was not encouraging; she seemed to have spoken to me out of a sense of duty. I looked humbly at the great jars that stood like eastern guards at either side of the dark entrance to the stall and murmured, 'No, thank you.'

The young lady changed the position of one of the vases and went back to the two young men. They began to talk of the same subject. Once or twice the young lady glanced at me over her shoulder.

I lingered before her stall, though I knew my stay was useless, to make my interest in her wares seem the more real. Then I turned away slowly and walked down the middle of the bazaar. I allowed the two pennies to fall against the sixpence in my pocket. I heard a voice call from one end of the gallery that the light was out. The upper part of the hall was now completely dark.

Gazing up into the darkness I saw myself as a creature driven and derided by vanity; and my eyes burned with anguish and anger.

Starting-points

1. *Talk about why it was so important to the boy that he should go to the Araby bazaar. Look carefully at how the writer describes the visit and note the ways that his actual experiences are different from what he had imagined.*

2. *Working in groups, adapt part of the story as a radio play. Start from where Mangan's sister first talks to the boy and end where he sets off for the bazaar. Try to capture the feelings of people in the words they use.*

3. *Make a list of words and phrases the writer uses to give precise descriptions of, for example, the night, the weather, the house. Then list some of the ways that Mangan's sister is described. Is her image more important to the boy than the person she actually is? How important are imagination and romance in everyone's lives?*

Suggestions for Writing

A. *Write a modern version of the story, set in your own community, about a boy or girl who is disappointed by a visit to a pop festival or a fairground.*

B. *Give a vivid account of the boy's experience at the bazaar and say whether you think this would change his relationship with Mangan's sister. Or write a sequel to the story which includes their next meeting.*

SUPERMAN AND PAULA BROWN'S NEW SNOWSUIT

Sylvia Plath

THE year the war began I was in the fifth grade at the Annie F. Warren Grammar School in Winthrop, and that was the winter I won the prize for drawing the best Civil Defence signs. That was also the winter of Paula Brown's new snowsuit, and even now, thirteen years later, I can recall the changing colours of those days, clear and definite as patterns seen through a kaleidoscope.

I lived on the bay side of town, on Johnson Avenue, opposite the Logan Airport, and before I went to bed each night, I used to kneel by the west window of my room and look over to the lights of Boston that blazed and blinked far off across the darkening water. The sunset flaunted its pink flag above the airport, and the sound of waves was lost in the perpetual droning of the planes. I marvelled at the moving beacons on the runway and watched, until it grew completely dark, the flashing red and green lights that rose and set in the sky like shooting stars. The airport was my Mecca, my Jerusalem. All night I dreamed of flying.

Those were the days of my technicolour dreams. Mother believed that I should have an enormous amount of sleep, and so I was never really tired when I went to bed. This was the best time of the day, when I could lie in the vague twilight, drifting off to sleep, making up dreams inside my head the way they should go. My flying dreams were believable as a landscape by Dali, so real that I would awake with a sudden shock, a breathless sense of having tumbled like Icarus from the sky and caught myself on the soft bed just in time.

These nightly adventures in space began when Superman started invading my dreams and teaching me how to fly. He used to come roaring by in his shining blue suit with his cape whistling in the wind, looking remarkably like my Uncle Frank who was living with

48

Mother and me. In the magic whirring of his cape I could hear the wings of a hundred sea-gulls, the motors of a thousand planes.

I was not the only worshipper of Superman in our block. David Sterling, a pale, bookish boy who lived down the street, shared my love for the sheer poetry of flight. Before supper every night, we listened to Superman together on the radio, and during the day we made up our own adventures on the way to school.

The Annie F. Warren Grammar School was a red-brick building, set back from the main highway on a black tar street, surrounded by barren gravel playgrounds. Out by the parking lot David and I found a perfect alcove for our Superman dramas. The dingy back entrance to the school was deep set in a long passageway which was an excellent place for surprise captures and sudden rescues.

During recess, David and I came into our own. We ignored the boys playing baseball on the gravel court and the girls giggling at dodge-ball in the dell. Our Superman games made us outlaws, yet gave us a sense of windy superiority. We even found a stand-in for a villain in Sheldon Fein, the sallow mamma's boy on our block who was left out of the boys' games because he cried whenever anybody tagged him and always managed to fall down and skin his fat knees.

At first, we had to prompt Sheldon in his part, but after a while he became an expert on inventing tortures and even carried them out in private, beyond the game. He used to pull the wings from flies and the legs off grasshoppers, and keep the broken insects captive in a jar hidden under his bed where he could take them out in secret and watch them struggling. David and I never played with Sheldon except at recess. After school we left him to his mamma, his bonbons, and his helpless insects.

At this time my Uncle Frank was living with us while waiting to be drafted, and I was sure that he bore an extraordinary resemblance to Superman incognito. David couldn't see his likeness as clearly as I did, but he admitted that Uncle Frank was the strongest man he had ever known, and could do lots of tricks like making caramels disappear under napkins and walking on his hands.

That same winter war was declared, and I remember sitting by the radio with Mother and Uncle Frank and feeling a queer foreboding in the air. Their voices were low and serious, and their talk was of planes and German bombs. Uncle Frank said something about Germans in America being put in prison for the duration, and Mother kept saying over and over again about Daddy, 'I'm only glad Otto didn't live to see this; I'm only glad Otto didn't live to see it come to this.'

In school we began to draw Civil Defence signs, and that was when I beat Jimmy Lane in our block for the fifth-grade prize. Every now and then we would practise an air raid. The fire bell would ring and we would take up our coats and pencils and file down the creaking stairs to the basement where we sat in special corners according to our colour tags, and put the pencils between our teeth so the bombs wouldn't make us bite our tongues by mistake. Some of the little children in the lower grades would cry because it was dark in the cellar, with only the bare ceiling lights on the cold black stone.

The threat of war was seeping in everywhere. At recess, Sheldon became a Nazi and borrowed a goose step from the movies, but his Uncle Macy was really over in Germany, and Mrs Fein began to grow thin and pale because she heard that Macy was a prisoner and then nothing more.

The winter dragged on, with a wet east wind coming always from the ocean, and the snow melting before there was enough for coasting. One Friday afternoon, just before Christmas, Paula Brown gave her annual birthday party, and I was invited because it was for all the children in our block. Paula lived across from Jimmy Lane on Somerset Terrace, and nobody on our block really liked her because she was bossy and stuck-up, with pale skin and long red pigtails and watery blue eyes.

She met us at the door of her house in a white organdie dress, her red hair tied up in sausage curls with a satin bow. Before we could sit down at the table for birthday cake and ice cream, she had to show us all her presents. There were a great many because it was both her birthday and Christmas time too.

Paula's favourite present was a new snowsuit, and she tried it on for us. The snowsuit was powder blue and came in a silver box from Sweden, she said. The front of the jacket was all embroidered with pink and white roses and blue-birds, and the leggings had em-broidered straps. She even had a little white angora beret and angora mittens to go with it.

After dessert we were all driven to the movies by Jimmy Lane's father to see the late afternoon show as a special treat. Mother had found out that the main feature was *Snow White* before she would let me go, but she hadn't realised that there was a war picture playing with it.

The movie was about Japanese prisoners who were being tortured by having no food or water. Our war games and the radio pro-grammes were all made up, but this was real, this really happened. I blocked my ears to shut out the groans of the thirsty, starving men, but I could not tear my eyes away from the screen.

Finally, the prisoners pulled down a heavy log from the low rafters and jammed it through the clay wall so they could reach the fountain in the court, but just as the first man got to the water, the Japanese began shooting the prisoners dead, and stamping on them, and laughing. I was sitting on the aisle, and I stood up then in a hurry and ran out to the girls' room where I knelt over a toilet bowl and vomited up the cake and ice cream.

After I went to bed that night, as soon as I closed my eyes, the prison camp sprang to life in my mind, and again the groaning men broke through the walls, and again they were shot down as they reached the trickling fountain. No matter how hard I thought of Superman before I went to sleep, no crusading blue figure came roaring down in heavenly anger to smash the yellow men who invaded my dreams. When I woke up in the morning, my sheets were damp with sweat.

Saturday was bitterly cold, and the skies were grey and blurred with the threat of snow. I was dallying home from the store that afternoon, curling up my chilled fingers in my mittens, when I saw a couple of kids playing Chinese tag out in front of Paula Brown's house.

Paula stopped in the middle of the game to eye me coldly. 'We need someone else,' she said. 'Want to play?' She tagged me on the ankle then, and I hopped around and finally caught Sheldon Fein as he was bending down to fasten one of his fur-lined overshoes. An early thaw had melted away the snow in the street, and the tarred pavement was gritted with sand left from the snow trucks. In front of Paula's house somebody's car had left a glittering black stain of oil-slick.

We went running about in the street, retreating to the hard, brown lawns when the one who was 'It' came too close. Jimmy Lane came out of his house and stood watching us for a short while, and then joined in. Every time he was 'It', he chased Paula in her powder blue snowsuit, and she screamed shrilly and looked around at him with her wide, watery eyes, and he always managed to catch her.

Only one time she forgot to look where she was going, and as Jimmy reached out to tag her, she slid into the oil-slick. We all froze when she went down on her side as if we were playing statues. No one said a word, and for a minute there was only the sound of the planes across the bay. The dull, green light of late afternoon came closing down on us, cold and final as a window blind.

51

Paula's snowsuit was smeared wet and black with oil along the side. Her angora mittens were dripping like black cat's fur. Slowly, she sat up and looked at us standing around her, as if searching for something. Then, suddenly, her eyes fixed on me.

'You,' she said deliberately, pointing at me, 'you pushed me.'

There was another second of silence, and then Jimmy Lane turned on me. 'You did it,' he taunted. 'You did it.'

Sheldon and Paula and Jimmy and the rest of them faced me with a strange joy flickering in the back of their eyes. 'You did it, you pushed her,' they said.

And even when I shouted 'I did not!' they were all moving in on me, chanting in a chorus, 'Yes, you did, yes, you did, we saw you.' In the well of faces moving toward me I saw no help, and I began to wonder if Jimmy had pushed Paula, or if she had fallen by herself, and I was not sure. I wasn't sure at all.

I started walking past them, walking home, determined not to run, but when I had left them behind me, I felt the sharp thud of a snowball on my left shoulder, and another. I picked up a faster stride and rounded the corner by Kelly's.

There was my dark brown shingled house ahead of me, and inside, Mother and Uncle Frank, home on furlough. I began to run in the cold, raw evening toward the bright squares of light in the windows that were home.

Uncle Frank met me at the door. 'How's my favourite trooper?' he asked, and he swung me so high in the air that my head grazed the ceiling. There was a big love in his voice that drowned out the shouting which still echoed in my ears.

'I'm fine,' I lied, and he taught me some ju-jitsu in the living-room until Mother called us for supper.

Candles were set on the white linen table-cloth, and miniature flames flickered in the silver and the glasses. I could see another room reflected beyond the dark dining-room window where the people laughed and talked in a secure web of light, held together by its indestructible brilliance.

All at once the doorbell rang, and Mother rose to answer it. I could hear David Sterling's high, clear voice in the hall. There was a cold draught from the open doorway, but he and Mother kept on talking, and he did not come in. When Mother came back to the table, her face was sad. 'Why didn't you tell me?' she said, 'why didn't you tell me that you pushed Paula in the mud and spoiled her new snow-suit?'

A mouthful of chocolate pudding blocked my throat, thick and bitter. I had to wash it down with milk. Finally I said, 'I didn't do it.'

But the words came out like hard, dry little seeds, hollow and insincere. I tried again. 'I didn't do it. Jimmy Lane did it.'

'Of course we'll believe you,' Mother said slowly, 'but the whole neighbourhood is talking about it. Mrs Sterling heard the story from Mrs Fein and sent David over to say we should buy Paula a new snowsuit. I can't understand it.'

'I didn't do it,' I repeated, and the blood beat in my ears like a slack drum. I pushed my chair away from the table, not looking at Uncle Frank or Mother sitting there, solemn and sorrowful in the candle-light.

The staircase to the second floor was dark, but I went down to the long hall to my room without turning on the light switch and shut the door. A small unripe moon was shafting squares of greenish light along the floor and the window-panes were fringed with frost.

I threw myself fiercely down on my bed and lay there, dry-eyed and burning. After a while I heard Uncle Frank coming up the stairs and knocking on my door. When I didn't answer, he walked in and sat down on my bed. I could see his strong shoulders bulk against the moonlight, but in the shadows his face was featureless.

'Tell me, Honey,' he said very softly, 'tell me. You don't have to be afraid. We'll understand. Only tell me how it really happened.'

'I told you,' I said. 'I told you what happened, and I can't make it any different. Not even for you I can't make it any different.'

He sighed then and got up to go away. 'O.K., Honey,' he said at the door. 'O.K., but we'll pay for another snowsuit anyway just to make everybody happy, and ten years from now no one will ever know the difference.'

The door shut behind him and I could hear his footsteps growing fainter as he walked off down the hall. I lay there alone in bed, feeling the black shadow creeping up the underside of the world like a flood tide. Nothing held, nothing was left. The silver airplanes and the blue capes all dissolved and vanished, wiped away like the crude drawings of a child in coloured chalk from the colossal black-board of the dark. That was the year the war began, and the real world, and the difference.

Starting-points

1. *Discuss the way the adults behave after David Sterling rings the doorbell. How does the girl know that the people she loves and respects do not believe her story? How does this make her feel? Talk about times when you thought adults did not believe you.*

2. *Talk about Uncle Frank and whether he lives up to the girl's expectations of him. Talk about the heroes you had when you were younger and any you have now. Are heroes important to everybody?*

3. *Working in pairs, develop a scene where one person accuses the other of something he or she has not done. The other person gives his version of what happened and is not believed. Talk about how you feel and how the girl in the story felt. Write out your scene as a script for a play.*

4. *The girl enjoys the security of the dreams she makes up inside her head and the safe Superman adventures she plays. She also experiences for the first time pain, deceit, injustice and cruelty. Note carefully what kinds of pain she feels. Discuss whether you think everyone has to go through similar experiences.*

Suggestions for Writing

A. *'Ten years from now no one will ever know the difference,' says Uncle Frank. Write a conversation that occurred ten years later between the girl and any other person in the story.*

B. *Describe the parts played in the story by Sheldon, Paula and Jimmy. What kinds of people are they? What makes each of them lie about who spoiled the snowsuit?*

C. *Write about a time when you told a lie, why you told it, how you felt, and what effect it had on other people. Or write about a time you were blamed for something you did not do.*

PITY
Frank O'Connor

DENIS'S school was in the heart of the country miles from anywhere, and this gave the teachers an initial advantage, because
before a boy even got to the railway station he had the prefects on his
track. Two fellows Denis knew once got as far as Mellin, a town ten
miles off, intending to join the British Army, but like fools the first
thing they did in Mellin was to go to a hotel, so they were caught in
bed in the middle of the night by prefects and brought back. It was
reported that they had been flogged on their knees in front of the
picture of the Crucifixion in the hall, but no one was ever able to find
out the truth about that. Denis thought they must have been in-
spired by the legend of two fellows who did once actually get on a
boat for England and were never heard of afterwards, but that was
before his time, and in those days escapes were probably easier. By
the time he got there it was said there was a telescope mounted on
the tower and that the prefects took turns at watching for fellows
trying to get away.

You could understand that, of course, for the fellows were all
rough, the sons of small farmers who smoked and gambled and took
a drink whenever they got a chance of one. As his mother said, it
wasn't a good school, but what could she do, and the small allow-
ance she got from his father? By this time she and his father were
living apart.

But one day a new boy came up and spoke to Denis. His name was
Francis Cummins and he came from Dunmore where Denis's
mother was now living. He wasn't in the least like the other fellows.
He was a funny, solemn kid with a head that was too big for his body
and a great flow of talk. It seemed that his people intended him for
the priesthood, and you could see that he'd make a good sort of
priest for he never wanted to do anything wrong, like breaking out,
or smoking, or playing cards, and he was a marvel at music. You had
only to whistle a tune to him and he could play it after on the piano.

Even the toughs in school let Francis alone. He was a fellow you couldn't get into a wax, no matter how you tried. He took every insult with a smile as if he couldn't believe you were serious, so that there was no satisfaction in trying to make him mad. And from the first day he almost pursued Denis. The other fellows in Denis's gang did not like it because if he saw them doing anything they shouldn't be doing he started at once to lecture them, exactly like a prefect, but somehow Denis found it impossible to quarrel with him. It was funny the way you felt to a fellow from your own place in a school like that, far from everywhere. And they did not know the feeling that came over Denis at times when he thought of Dunmore and his home and Martha, for all that he was forever fighting with her. Sometimes he would dream of it at night, and wake up thinking of it, and all that day it would haunt him in snatches till he felt like throwing himself on his bed and bawling. And that wasn't possible either, with forty kids to a room and the beds packed tight in four rows.

There was also another reason for his toleration of a cissy like Cummins. Every week of Cummins's life he got a parcel from home, and it was always an astonishment to Denis, for his parents sent him tinned meat, tinned fruit, sardines and everything. Now, Denis was always hungry. The school food wasn't much at the best of times, and because his mother couldn't afford the extras, he never got rashers for breakfast as most of the others did. His father visited him regularly and kept on inquiring in a worried way if he was all right, but Denis had been warned not to complain to him, and the pound or two he gave Denis never lasted more than a couple of days. When he was not dreaming of home he dreamt of food. Cummins always shared his parcels with him, and when Denis grew ashamed of the way he cadged from Cummins, it was a sop to his conscience that Cummins seemed to enjoy it as much as he did. Cummins lectured him like an old schoolmistress, and measured it all out, down to that last candy.

'I'll give you one slice of cake now,' he would say in his cheerful argumentative way.

'Ah, come on!' Denis would growl, eyeing it hungrily. 'You won't take it with you.'

'But if I give it to you now you'll only eat it all,' Cummins would cry. 'Look, if I give you one slice now, and another slice tomorrow, and another on Sunday, you'll have cake three days instead of one.'

'But what good will that be if I'm still hungry?' Denis would shout.

'But you'll only be hungrier tomorrow night,' Cummins would

say in desperation at his greed, 'You're a queer fellow, Denis,' he would chatter on. 'You're always the same. 'Tis always a feast or a famine with you. If you had your own way you'd never have anything at all. You see I'm only speaking for your good, don't you?'

Denis had no objection to Cummins's speaking for his good so long as he got the cake, as he usually did. You could see from the way Cummins was always thinking of your good that he was bound to be a priest. Sometimes it went too far even for Denis, like the day the two of them were passing the priests' orchard and he suddenly saw that for once there wasn't a soul in sight. At the same moment he felt the hunger-pain sweep over him like a fever.

'Keep nix now, Cummins,' he said, beginning to shin up the wall.

'What are you going to do, Denis?' Cummins asked after him in a frenzy of anxiety.

'I only want a couple of apples,' Denis said, jumping from the top of the wall and running towards the trees. He heard a long, loud wail from the other side of the wall.

'Denis, you're not going to STEAL them. Don't steal them, Denis, please don't steal them!'

But by this time Denis was up in the fork of the tree where the biggest, reddest apples grew. He heard his name called again, and saw that Cummins had scrambled up on to the wall as well, and was sitting astride it with real tears in his eyes.

'Denis,' he bawled, 'what'll I say if I'm caught?'

'Shut up, you fool, or you will get us caught,' Denis snarled back at him.

'But Denis. Denis, it's a sin.'

'It's a what?'

'It's a sin, Denis. I know it's only a venial sin, but venial sins lead to mortal ones. Denis, I'll give you the rest of my cake if you come away. Honest, I will.'

Denis didn't bother to reply, but he was raging. He finished packing apples wherever he had room for them in his clothes, and then climbed slowly back over the wall.

'Cummins,' he said fiercely, 'if you do that again I'm going to kill you.'

'But it's true, Denis,' Cummins said, wringing his hands distractedly. ''Tis a sin, and you know 'tis a sin, and you'll have to tell it in Confession.'

'I will not tell it in Confession,' said Denis, 'and if I find out that you did, I'll kill you. I mean it.'

And he did, at the time. It upset him so much that he got almost

57

no pleasure from the apples, but he and Cummins still continued to be friends and to share the parcels of food that Cummins got. These were a complete mystery to Denis. None of the other fellows he knew got a parcel oftener than once a month, and Denis himself hardly got one a term. Of course, Cummins's parents kept a little shop so that it wouldn't be so much trouble to them, making up a parcel, and anyway they would get things at cost price, but even allowing for all this, it was still remarkable. If they cared all that much for Cummins, why didn't they keep him at home? It wasn't even as if he had another brother or sister. Himself, for instance, a wild kid who was always quarrelling with his sister and whose mother was so often away from home, he could see why he had to be sent away, but what had Cummins done to deserve it? There was a mystery here, and when he got home, Denis was determined to investigate it.

He had his first opportunity at the end of term when Cummins's father and mother came for him in a car and brought Denis back as well. Old Cummins was a small man with glasses and a little greying moustache, and his wife was a roly-poly of a woman with a great flow of talk. Denis noticed the way Cummins's father would wait for minutes on end to ask a question of his own. Cummins's manner to them was affectionate enough. He seemed to have no self-consciousness, and would turn round with one leg on the front seat to hold his mother's hand while he answered her questions about the priests.

A week later, Martha and Denis went up to the Cumminses' for tea. Mr Cummins was behind the counter of the shop with his hat on his head, and he called his wife from the foot of the stairs. She brought them upstairs in her excitable, chattering way to a big front room over the street. Denis and Cummins went out to the back garden with a pistol that Cummins had got at Christmas. It was a wonderful air-pistol that Denis knew must have cost pounds. All Cummins's things were like that. He had also been given a piano accordion. Denis did not envy him the accordion, but he did passionately want the pistol.

'Lend it to us anyway, for the holidays,' he begged.

'But, sure, when I want to practise with it myself!' Cummins protested in that babyish way of his.

'What do you want to practise with it for?' asked Denis. 'When you're a priest, you won't be able to shoot.'

'How do you know?' asked Cummins.

'Because priests aren't let shoot anybody,' said Denis.

'I'll tell you what I'll do with you,' Cummins said in his usual cheese-paring way, 'I'll keep it on weekdays and you can have it on Saturday and Sunday.'

Denis didn't want it for Saturday and Sunday; he wanted it for keeps; and it struck him as very queer in a cissy like Cummins, being so attached to a gun that he'd be scared to use.

Mrs Cummins and the three children had tea in the front room. Then Cummins and Martha played the piano while Mrs Cummins talked to Denis about school.

'Wisha, Denis,' she said, 'isn't it wonderful for ye to be going to a beautiful school like that?'

Denis thought she was joking and began to smile.

'And the grounds so lovely and the house so lovely inside. Don't you love the stained-glass window in the hall?'

Denis had never particularly noticed the stained glass, but he vaguely remembered it as she spoke and agreed.

'Ah, sure 'tis lovely, with the chapel there, to go to whenever you like. And Francis says ye have the grandest films?'

'Oh yes,' said Denis, thinking he would prefer threepenceworth at the local cinema any day of the week.

'And 'tis so nice having priests for teachers in place of the rough, coarse country fellows you have around here. Oh, Denis, I'm crazy about Father Murphy. Do you know, I'm sure that man is a saint.'

'He's very holy,' said Denis, wondering whether Mrs Cummins would think Murphy such a saint if she saw him with a cane in his hand and his face the colour of blood, hissing and snarling as he chased some fellow round the class-room, flogging him on his bare legs.

'Oh, to be sure he is,' Mrs Cummins rattled on. 'And 'tisn't that at all, Denis boy, but the nice, gentlemanly friends you can make there instead of the savages there are in this town. Look, 'tisn't wishing to me to have Francis out of my sight with those brutes around the streets.'

That finished Denis. A fellow would be a long time in Dunmore before he met savages like the two Corbetts from Cork or Barrett from Clare. But he saw that the woman was in earnest. When he returned home, he told his mother everything about their visit, and her amusement convinced him of what he had already suspected – that Mrs Cummins didn't know any better. She and her husband, small shopkeepers who were accustomed only to a little house in a terrace, nearly died with the grandeur when they saw the grounds and the lake and the tennis-courts, just like the gentlemen's

59

residences they had seen before that only from the roadway. Of course, they thought it was Heaven. And it explained the mystery about Francis, because, in place of wanting to get rid of him as his mother had to get rid of Denis, they were probably breaking their hearts at having to part with him at all, and doing it only because they felt they were giving him all the advantages that had been denied to themselves. Despite his mother's mockery he felt rather sorry for them, being taken in like that by appearances.

At the same time it left unexplained something about Francis himself. Denis knew that if he was an only child with a mother and father like that, he would not allow them to remain in ignorance for long. He would soon get away from the filthy dormitory and the brutal society. At first he thought that Francis probably thought it a fine place too, and in a frenzy of altruism decided that it was his duty to talk to Mrs Cummins and tell her the whole truth about it, but then he realised that Francis could not possibly have been taken in in the same way as his parents. He was a weakling and a prig, but he had a sort of country cuteness which enabled him to see through fellows. No, Francis was probably putting up with it because he felt it was his duty, or for the sake of his vocation, because he thought that life was like that, a vale of tears, and whenever he was homesick or when fellows jeered at him, he probably went to the chapel and offered it up. It seemed very queer to Denis because when he was homesick or mad he waited till lights were out and then started to bawl in complete silence for fear his neighbours would hear.

He made a point of impressing on his mother the lavishness of the Cumminses, and told her all about the accordion and the pistol and the weekly parcels with a vague hope of creating larger standards of generosity in her, but she only said that Irish shopkeepers were rotten with money and didn't know how to spend it, and that if only Denis's father would give her what she was entitled to he might go to the best college in Ireland where he would meet only the children of professional people.

All the same, when he went back to school there was a change. A parcel arrived for him, and when he opened it there were all the things he had mentioned to her. For a while he felt a little ashamed. It was probably true that his father did not give her all the money she needed, and that she could only send him parcels by stinting herself; but still, it was a relief to be able to show off in front of the others whose parents were less generous.

That evening he ran into Cummins who smiled at him in his pudding-faced way.

'Do you want anything, Denis?' he asked. 'I have a parcel if you do.'

'I have a parcel of my own today,' Denis said cockily. 'Would you like peaches? I have peaches.'

'Don't be eating it all now,' Cummins said with a comic wail. 'You won't have anything left tomorrow if you do.'

'Ah, what difference does it make?' said Denis with a shrug, and with reckless abandonment he rewarded his friends and conciliated his foes with the contents of his parcel. Next evening he was almost as bad as ever.

'Jay, Denis,' Cummins said with amused resignation, 'you're a blooming fright. I told you what was going to happen. How are you going to live when you grow up if you can never keep anything?'

'Ah, boy,' Denis said, in his embarrassment doing the big shot, 'you wait till I am grown up and you'll see.'

'I know what I'll see all right,' Cummins said, shaking his head sadly. 'Better men than you went to the wall. 'Tis the habits we learn at this age that decide what we're going to be later on. And anyway, how are you going to get a job? Sure, you won't learn anything. If you'd even learn the piano I could teach you.'

Cummins was a born preacher, and Denis saw that there was something in what he said, but no amount of preaching could change him. That was the sort he was. Come day, go day, God send Sunday – and anyway it didn't really make much difference because Cummins with his thrifty habits usually had enough to keep him going till the next parcel came.

Then, about a month later as Denis was opening his weekly parcel under the eyes of his gang, Anthony Harty stood by, gaping with the rest. Harty was a mean, miserable creature from Clare who never got anything, and was consumed with jealousy of everyone who did.

'How well you didn't get any parcels last year, and now you're getting them all the time, Halligan,' he said suspiciously.

'That's only because my mother didn't know about the grub in this place,' Denis declared confidently.

'A wonder she wouldn't address them herself, so,' sneered Harty.

'What do you mean, Harty?' Denis asked, going up to him with his fists clenched. 'Are you looking for a puck in the gob?'

'I'm only saying that's not the writing on your letters,' replied Harty, pointing at the label.

'And why would it be?' shouted Denis. 'I suppose it could be the shopkeepers'.'

'That looks to me like the same writing as on Cummins's parcels,' said Harty.

'And what's wrong with that?' Denis asked, feeling a pang of terror. 'I suppose she could order them there, couldn't she?'

'I'm not saying she couldn't,' said Harty in his sulky, sneering tone, 'I'm only telling you what I think.'

Denis could not believe it, but at the same time he could get no further pleasure from the parcel. He put it back in his locker and went out by himself and skulked away among the trees. It was a dull, misty February day. He took out his wallet in which there was a picture of his mother and Martha, and two letters he had received from his mother. He read the letters through, but there was no reference to any parcel that she was sending. He still could not believe but that there was some simple explanation, and that she had intended the parcels as a surprise, but the very thought of the alternative made his heart turn over. It was something he could talk to nobody about, and after lights out, he twisted and turned madly, groaning at the violence of his own restlessness, and the more he turned, the clearer he saw that the parcels had come from the Cumminses and not from his mother.

He had never before felt so humiliated. Though he had not realised it he had been buoyed up less by the parcels than by the thought that his mother cared so much for him; he had been filled with a new love of her, and now all the love was turning back on him and he realised that he hated her. But he hated the Cumminses worse. He saw that he had pitied and patronised Francis Cummins because he was weak and priggish and because his parents were only poor, ignorant country shopkeepers who did not know a good school from a bad one, while they all the time had been pitying him because he had no one to care for him as the Cumminses cared for Francis. He could clearly imagine the three Cumminses discussing him, his mother and his father exactly as his mother and he had discussed them. The only difference was that however ignorant they might be they had been right. It was he and not Francis who deserved pity.

'What ails you, Halligan?' the chap in the next bed asked – the beds were ranked so close together that one couldn't even sob in peace.

'Nothing ails me,' Denis said between his teeth.

Next day he bundled up what remained of the parcel and took it to

62

Cummins's dormitory. He had intended just to leave it and walk out but Cummins was there himself, sitting on his bed with a book, and Denis had to say something.

'That's yours, Cummins,' he said. 'And if you ever do a thing like that again, I'll kill you.'

'What did I do, Denis?' Cummins wailed, getting up from his bed.

'You got your mother to send me that parcel.'

'I didn't. She did it herself.'

'But you told her to. Who asked you to interfere in my business, you dirty spy?'

'I'm not a spy,' Cummins said, growing agitated. 'You needed it and I didn't – what harm is there in that?'

'There is harm. Pretending my mother isn't as good as yours – a dirty old shopkeeper.'

'I wasn't, Denis,' Cummins said excitedly. 'Honest, I wasn't. I never said a word against your mother.'

'What did he do to you, Halligan?' one of the fellows asked, affecting to take Cummins's part.

'He got his people to send me parcels, as if I couldn't get them myself if I wanted them,' Denis shouted, losing control of himself. 'I don't want his old parcels.'

'Well, that's nothing to cry about.'

'Who's crying?' shouted Denis. 'I'm not crying. I'll fight him and you and the best man in the dormitory.'

He waited a moment for someone to take up his challenge, but they only looked at him curiously, and he rushed out because he knew that in spite of himself he was crying. He went straight to the lavatory and had his cry out there on the seat. It was the only place they had to cry, the only one where there was some sort of privacy. He cried because he had thought he was keeping his secret so well and that no one but himself knew how little toughness and insubordination there was in him till Cummins had come and pried it out.

After that he could never be friendly with Cummins again. It wasn't as Cummins thought that he bore a grudge. It was merely that for him it would have been like living naked.

Starting-points

1. In pairs, act out the scene where Denis opens his food parcel and Anthony Harty watches. What are Denis's feelings at this time?

2. Towards the end of the story Denis imagines how the Cumminses discussed him. Working in threes, take the parts of Francis, his mother and his father. Use what you know of each character to develop the conversation that Denis imagined.

3. From the very first paragraph Denis is interested in breaking out of school. Talk about those features of school life that make him feel this way. How much is due to the kind of person Denis is?

Suggestions for Writing

A. Imagine Denis does try to break out after the events of this story. Cummins is asked to explain if he knows why Denis tried to run away. Write an explanation to Father Murphy in the way Cummins would have given it.

B. Compare and contrast Denis and Francis Cummins. What kinds of people are they? What are their outlooks on life? Trace the stages of their relationship with each other and decide what each learned from this. Do you pity either of them? Discuss whether it is always difficult to help someone you pity.

C. Look again at the part where Denis steals apples and decide why Cummins behaves as he does. Write a short play script in which you try to stop someone doing something that you believe is wrong.

THE FOLLOWERS

Dylan Thomas

IT was six o'clock on a winter's evening. Thin, dingy rain spat and drizzled past the lighted street lamps. The pavements shone long and yellow. In squeaking galoshes, with mackintosh collars up and bowlers and trilbies weeping, youngish men from the offices bundled home against the thistly wind –

'Night, Mr Macey.'

'Going my way, Charlie?'

'Ooh, there's a pig of a night!'

'Good night, Mr Swan.' –

and older men, clinging on to the big, black circular birds of their umbrellas, were wafted back, up the gaslit hills, to safe, hot slippered, weather-proof hearths, and wives called Mother, and old, fond, fleabag dogs, and the wireless babbling.

Young women from the offices, who smelt of scent and powder and wet pixie hoods and hair, scuttled, giggling, arm in arm, after the hissing trams, and screeched as they splashed their stockings in the puddles rainbowed with oil between the slippery lines.

In a shop window, two girls undressed the dummies:

'Where you going tonight?'

'Depends on Arthur. Up she comes.'

'Mind her camiknicks, Edna. . . .'

The blinds came down over another window.

A newsboy stood in a doorway, calling the news to nobody, very softly, 'Earthquake. Earthquake in Japan'.

Water from a chute dripped on to his sacking. He waited in his own pool of rain.

A flat, long girl drifted, snivelling into her hanky, out of a jeweller's shop, and slowly pulled the steel shutters down with a hooked pole. She looked, in the grey rain, as though she were crying from top to toe.

A silent man and woman, dressed in black, carried the wreaths away from the front of their flower shop into the scented deadly darkness behind the window lights. Then the lights went out.

A man with a balloon tied to his cap pushed a shrouded barrow up a dead end.

A baby with an ancient face sat in its pram outside the wine vaults, quiet, very wet, peering cautiously all round it.

It was the saddest evening I had ever known.

A young man, with his arm round his girl, passed by me, laughing; and she laughed back, right into his handsome, nasty face. That made the evening sadder still.

I met Leslie at the corner of Crimea Street. We were both about the same age: too young and too old. Leslie carried a rolled umbrella, which he never used, though sometimes he pressed doorbells with it. He was trying to grow a moustache. I wore a check ratting cap at a Saturday angle. We greeted each other formally:

'Good evening, old man.'

'Evening, Leslie.'

'Right on the dot, boy.'

'That's right,' I said. 'Right on the dot.'

A plump, blonde girl, smelling of wet rabbits, self-conscious even in that dirty night, minced past on high-heeled shoes. The heels clicked, the soles squelched.

Leslie whistled after her, low and admiring.

'Business first,' I said.

'Oh boy!' Leslie said.

'And she's too fat as well.'

'I like them corpulent,' Leslie said. 'Remember Penelope Bogan? A Mrs too.'

'Oh, come *on*. That old bird of Paradise Alley! How's the exchequer, Les?'

'One and a penny. How you fixed?'

'Tanner.'

'What'll it be, then? The Compasses?'

'Free cheese at the Marlborough.'

We walked towards the Marlborough, dodging umbrella spokes, smacked by our windy macs, stained by steaming lamplight, seeing the sodden, blown scourings and street-wash of the town, papers, rags, dregs, rinds, fag-ends, balls of fur, flap, float and cringe along the gutters, hearing the sneeze and rattle of the bony trams and a ship hoot like a fog-ditched owl in the bay, and Leslie said, 'What'll we do after?'

'We'll follow someone,' I said.

'Remember following that old girl up Kitchener Street? The one who dropped her handbag?'

'You should have given it back.'

'There wasn't anything in it, only a piece of bread and jam.'

'Here we are,' I said.

The Marlborough saloon was cold and empty. There were notices on the damp walls: No Singing. No Dancing. No Gambling. No Peddlers.

'You sing,' I said to Leslie, 'and I'll dance, then we'll have a game of nap and I'll peddle my braces.'

The barmaid, with gold hair and two gold teeth in front, like a well-off rabbit's, was blowing on her nails and polishing them on her black marocain. She looked up as we came in, then blew on her nails again and polished them without hope.

'You can tell it isn't Saturday night,' I said. 'Evening, miss. Two pints.'

'And a pound from the till,' Leslie said.

'Give us your one and a penny, Les,' I whispered, and then said aloud, 'Anybody can tell it isn't Saturday night. Nobody sick.'

'Nobody here to *be* sick,' Leslie said.

The peeling, liver-coloured room might never have been drunk in at all. Here, commercials told jokes and had Scotches and sodas with happy, dyed, port-and-lemon women; dejected regulars grew grand and muzzy in the corners, inventing their pasts, being rich, important, and loved; reprobate grannies in dustbin black cackled and nipped; influential nobodies revised the earth; a party, with ear-rings, called 'Frilly Willy' played the crippled piano, which sounded like a hurdy-gurdy playing under water, until the publican's nosy wife said 'No'. Strangers came and went, but mostly went. Men from the valleys dropped in for nine or ten; sometimes there were fights; and always there was something doing, some argy-bargy, giggle and bluster, horror or folly, affection, explosion, nonsense, peace, some wild goose flying in the boozy air of that comfortless, humdrum nowhere in the dizzy, ditch-water town at the end of the railway lines. But that evening it was the saddest room I had ever known.

Leslie said, in a low voice, 'Think she'll let us have one on tick?'

'Wait a bit, boy,' I murmured. 'Wait for her to thaw.'

But the barmaid heard me, and looked up. She looked clean through me, back through my small history to the bed I was born in, then shook her gold head.

'I don't know what it is,' said Leslie as we walked up Crimea Street in the rain, 'but I feel kind of depressed tonight.'

'It's the saddest night in the world,' I said.

We stopped, soaked and alone, to look at the stills outside the cinema we called the Itch-pit. Week after week, for years and years, we had sat on the edges of the springless seats there, in the dank but snug, flickering dark, first with toffees and monkey-nuts that crackled for the dumb guns, and then with cigarettes: a cheap special kind that would make a fire-swallower cough up the cinders of his heart. 'Let's go in and see Lon Chaney,' I said, 'and Richard Talmadge and Milton Sills and . . . Noah Beary,' I said, 'and Richard Dix . . . and Slim Summerville and Hoot Gibson.'

We both sighed.

'Oh for our vanished youth,' I said.

We walked on heavily, with wilful feet, splashing the passers-by.

'Why don't you open your brolly?' I said.

'It won't open. You try.'

We both tried, and the umbrella suddenly bellied out, the spokes tore through the soaking cover; the wind danced its tatters; it wrangled above us in the wind like a ruined, mathematical bird. We tried to tug it down: an unseen, new spoke sprang through its ragged ribs. Leslie dragged it behind him, along the pavement, as though he had shot it.

A girl called Dulcie, scurrying to the Itch-pit, sniggered 'Hullo', and we stopped her.

'A rather terrible thing has happened,' I said to her. She was so silly that, even when she was fifteen, we had told her to eat soap to make her straw hair crinkle, and Les took a piece from the bathroom, and she did.

'I know,' she said, 'you broke your gamp.'

'No, you're wrong there,' Leslie said. 'It isn't *our* umbrella at all. It fell off the roof. *You* feel,' he said. 'You can feel it fell off the roof.' She took the umbrella gingerly by its handle.

'There's someone up there throwing umbrellas down,' I said. 'It may be serious.'

She began to titter, and then grew silent and anxious as Leslie said, 'You never know. It might be walking-sticks next.'

'Or sewing-machines,' I said.

'You wait here, Dulce, and we'll investigate,' Leslie said.

We hurried on down the street, turned a blowing corner, and then ran.

Outside Rabiotti's café, Leslie said, 'It isn't fair on Dulcie.' We never mentioned it again.

A wet girl brushed by. Without a word, we followed her. She cantered, long-legged, down Inkerman Street and through Paradise Passage, and we were at her heels.

'I wonder what's the point in following people,' Leslie said. 'It's kind of daft. It never gets you anywhere. All you do is follow them home and then try to look through the window and see what they're doing and mostly there's curtains anyway. I bet nobody else does things like that.'

'You never know,' I said. The girl turned into St Augustus Crescent, which was a wide lamplit mist. 'People are always following people. What shall we call her?'

'Hermione Weatherby,' Leslie said. He was never wrong about names. Hermione was fey and stringy, and walked like a long gym-mistress, full of love, through the stinging rain.

'You never know. You never know what you'll find out. Perhaps she lives in a huge house with all her sisters – '

'How many?'

'Seven. All full of love. And when she gets home they all change into kimonos and lie on divans with music and whisper to each other and all they're doing is waiting for somebody like us to walk in, lost, and then they'll all chatter round us like starlings and put us in kimonos too, and we'll never leave the house until we die. Perhaps it's so beautiful and soft and noisy – like a warm bath full of birds. . . .'

'I don't want birds in my bath,' said Leslie. 'Perhaps she'll slit her throat if they don't draw the blinds. I don't care what happens so long as it's interesting.'

She slip-slopped round a corner into an avenue where the neat trees were sighing and the cosy windows shone.

'I don't want old feathers in the tub,' Leslie said.

Hermione turned in at number thirteen, *Beach-view*.

'You can see the beach all right,' Leslie said, 'if you got a periscope.'

We waited on the pavement opposite, under a bubbling lamp, as Hermione opened her door, and then we tiptoed across and down the gravel path and were at the back of the house, outside an uncurtained window.

Hermione's mother, a round, friendly, owlish woman in a pinafore, was shaking a chip-pan on the kitchen stove.

'I'm hungry,' I said.

'Ssh!'

We edged to the side of the window as Hermione came into the kitchen. She was old, nearly thirty, with a mouse-brown shingle and big earnest eyes. She wore horn-rimmed spectacles and a sensible tweed costume, and a white shirt with a trim bow-tie. She looked as though she tried to look like a secretary in domestic films, who had only to remove her spectacles and have her hair cherished, and be dressed like silk dog's dinner, to turn into a dazzler and make her employer, Warner Baxter, gasp, woo, and marry her; but if Hermione took off her glasses, she wouldn't be able to tell if he was Warner Baxter or the man who read the meters.

We stood so near the window, we could hear the chips spitting.

'Have a nice day in the office, dear? There's weather,' Hermione's mother said, worrying the chip-pan.

'What's *her* name, Les?'

'Hetty.'

Everything there in the warm kitchen, from the tea-caddy and the grandmother clock, to the tabby that purred like a kettle, was good, dull and sufficient.

'Mr Truscot was something awful,' Hermione said as she put on her slippers.

'Where's her kimono?' Leslie said.

'Here's a nice cup of tea,' said Hetty.

'Everything's nice in that old hole,' said Leslie, grumbling. 'Where's the seven sisters like starlings?'

It began to rain much more heavily. It bucketed down on the black backyard, and the little comfy kennel of a house, and us, and the hidden, hushed town, where, even now, in the haven of the Marlborough, the submarine piano would be tinning 'Daisy', and the happy henna'd women squealing into their port.

Hetty and Hermione had their supper. Two drowned boys watched them enviously.

'Put a drop of Worcester on the chips,' Leslie whispered; and by God she did.

'Doesn't anything happen anywhere?' I said. 'In the whole wide world? I think the *News of the World* is all made up. Nobody murders no one. There isn't any sin any more, or love, or death, or pearls and divorces and mink coats or anything, or putting arsenic in the cocoa. . . .'

'Why don't they put on some music for us,' Leslie said, 'and do a dance? It isn't every night they got two fellows watching them in the rain. Not *every* night, anyway!'

All over the dripping town, small lost people with nowhere to go and nothing to spend were gooseberrying in the rain outside wet windows, but nothing happened.

'I'm getting pneumonia,' Leslie said.

The cat and the fire were purring, grandmother time tick-tocked our lives away. The supper was cleared, and Hetty and Hermione,

70

who had not spoken for many minutes, they were so confident and close in their little lighted box, looked at one another and slowly smiled.

They stood still in the decent, purring kitchen, facing one another.

'There's something funny going to happen,' I whispered very softly.

'It's going to begin,' Leslie said.

We did not notice the sour, racing rain any more.

The smiles stayed on the faces of the two still, silent women.

'It's going to begin.'

And we heard Hetty say in a small secret voice, 'Bring out the album, dear.'

Hermione opened a cupboard and brought out a big, stiff-coloured photograph album, and put it in the middle of the table. Then she and Hetty sat down at the table, side by side, and Hermione opened the album.

'That's Uncle Eliot who died in Porthcawl, the one who had the cramp,' said Hetty.

They looked with affection at Uncle Eliot, but we could not see him.

'That's Martha-the-woolshop, you wouldn't remember her, dear, it was wool, wool, wool, with her all the time; she wanted to be buried in her jumper, the mauve one, but her husband put his foot down. He'd been in India. That's your Uncle Morgan,' Hetty said, 'one of the Kidwelly Morgans, remember him in the snow?'

Hermione turned a page. 'And that's Myfanwy, she got queer all of a sudden, remember. It was when she was milking. That's your cousin Jim, the Minister, until they found out. And that's our Beryl,' Hetty said.

But she spoke all the time like somebody repeating a lesson: a well-loved lesson she knew by heart.

We knew that she and Hermione were only waiting.

Then Hermione turned another page. And we knew, by their secret smiles, that this was what they had been waiting for.

'My sister Katinka,' Hetty said.

'Auntie Katinka,' Hermione said. They bent over the photograph.

'Remember that day in Aberystwyth, Katinka?' Hetty said softly. 'The day we went on the choir outing.'

'I wore my new white dress,' a new voice said.

Leslie clutched at my hand.

'And a straw hat with birds,' said the clear, new voice.

Hermione and Hetty were not moving their lips.

'I was always a one for birds on my hat. Just the plumes of course. It was August the third, and I was twenty-three.'

'Twenty-three come October, Katinka,' Hetty said.

'That's right, love,' the voice said. 'Scorpio I was. And we met Douglas Pugh on the Prom and he said, "You look like a queen today, Katinka," he said. "You look like a queen, Katinka," he said. Why are those two boys looking in at the window?'

We ran up the gravel drive, and around the corner of the house, and into the avenue and out on to St Augustus Crescent. The rain roared down to drown the town. There we stopped for breath. We did not speak or look at each other. Then we walked on through the rain. At Victoria corner, we stopped again.

'Good-night, old man,' Leslie said.

'Good-night,' I said.

And we went our different ways.

Starting-points

1. *'What's the point in following people,' Leslie says about the way they choose to relieve their boredom. What feelings and actions in the story seem to you to fit in well with your idea of adolescence? Talk about these and discuss whether everyone at the stage between youth and adulthood goes through similar experiences.*

2. *Look at the description at the beginning of the story of the 'saddest evening he's ever known'. List the things which make it sad. Note down the detailed observations that the writer makes which appeal to our senses (smell, sight, sound, touch, movement).*

3. *In small groups, rewrite the final episode in the kitchen as for a radio play. Remember your audience has to follow events and understand feelings through words and sounds alone. So choose these carefully. Record your version. Do you think the ending to the story is the best the writer could have given?*

Suggestions for Writing

A. *Describe the two youths in the story, drawing your evidence from what they do and what they say to one another as well as to other people. What kinds of people are they and what are their feelings in the story? Can you see any differences between them? What is your attitude towards them?*

B. *Using the notes you made for Starting-point 2, show how the writer's choice of detail vividly creates the mood of the story. Or describe your own street in a similarly detailed way, making the atmosphere either sad or happy.*

THE OPPOSITE SEX

Laurie Lee

IT wasn't the discovery of sex that affected my life so much as the first occasion that I met it head on.

I don't think I ever discovered sex, it seemed to be always there – a vague pink streak running back through the landscape as far as I can remember. This was probably due to my country upbringing, where life was open as a cucumber-frame, and sex a constant force like the national grid, occasionally boosted by thundery weather. There were the free, unpackaged animals and birds, constantly proving their tireless urges, all coolly encouraged and pandered to as one of the parish's more profitable drives. My childhood was cluttered with fumbling bees, loaded udders, and swelling fruit, with bellowing livestock, hypnotised hens, and bulls being led by the nose. Sex in the country was like grain in the wood, self-renewing as the daily paper, never obsessive, nor crowding the attention, but always going on if you cared to look for it.

So the twisted shock of a sudden sex-dawning was not a problem I was asked to bear. My moment, after years of lazily inspecting the pitch, came when I was suddenly called on to play. There had, of course, been early practice at the nets, some of it solitary, though not without promise. Then the occasion arrived when I actually stood at the crease, bat in hand, ready to strip the willow.

I couldn't have been more than fifteen at the time – I remember I had just left school. Our small Cotswold village was crammed with boys of my age, all coming to a head together – loose rangey lads, overgrown like weeds, top-heavy and multi-branched. We all seemed to steam or give off fumes like a furnace, heated more than we were wont to be heated, and as there were few cars or motorbikes to talk about, we were free to concentrate on sex.

Sex, and our questionable success at it, was the only status we sought, though virginity at that age, in spite of our boasted loss of it, was honoured more in the evasion than in the breach. So we squatted together in our rain-dark shed, painting the walls with our gaudy lies, playing competitive fantasies one against the other until we believed ourselves veterans.

Then one evening, walking home from one such gathering, I lost its cosy half-world for ever. In a field near the vicarage, in a moment of terror and truth, I was confronted by a whole live girl. She stood in the grass, supposedly unaware, twitching her eyes like a grazing animal, indolently angling her flanks to the hunter and closely watching me sideways.

I recognised her as a girl from a neighbouring village, a girl called Ellie, whom I'd known since a child. But she'd never directly looked at me before, and so I'd never really seen her. Seeing her now, brushing the grass with her hand, I was suddenly stung by brutish ambition. I thought of carrying this trophy back to the shed, laying it warm and real on the stones. I thought of the lads crowding round in a sudden miracle of silence. I also thought of Rudolph.

Rudolph was my closest friend at the time, and we used each other as whetstones. He was a year older than I; a thin, shifty lad who seemed specially constructed for scuttling down holes. We had competed together since we were infants and sucked the blood of each other's jealousies. Rudolph must see this, I thought to myself. He wouldn't believe it otherwise.

'Seen any snakes?' asked Ellie.

I made no reply, but strode past her, mournfully whistling. I was wearing my brother's plus-fours and woollen stockings and the grass bounced off my legs like blow-darts.

The next day I steered Rudolph up to the vicarage fields, and sure enough she was there again. But this time she was draped across the top of the stile so that there was no way of getting past her. She lay sprawled across it, her knees to her chin, a languorous and weighty road-block.

'Oo's 'er?' muttered Rudolph, pulling up fast.

'I dunno,' I said, on needles.

'Some Bisley bird. Let's clip 'er earhole.'

'O.K. Let's clip 'er earhole.'

Large, beautiful, with Spanish hair and eyes, skin tight with flesh as an apple, Ellie slipped from the stile and faced us boldly, smiling a slow, fat smile. I watched her closely as her eyes moved over us, heavy-lidded as a sleepy owl. Her lazy gaze finally rested on Rudolph. It was an excruciating moment of doubt.

'Push off, you,' she murmured.

Rudolph didn't argue; he gave a thin dry cough and went.

I was alone with the girl in a smell of warm rain, feeling hand-some, jaunty and chosen. Ellie stood thigh-deep in the glittering grass like a half-submerged tropic idol.

'Lift us up on that wall, come on,' she said. 'I'm dead scared of things in the grass.'

My hands sunk deep into her open armpits and she rose in the air like a bird. I wouldn't have believed it, or that I could do it, it was like lifting a healthy eagle.

The flat stone wall, backed by a twisted beech, seemed wider than any bed. We lay cradled together in its dusty silence looking down at the running grass.

"Ow's yer cousin?' said Ellie. 'We've 'ad some laughs. 'Er an' me. We thought we'd choke.'

One side of my body was hot against her, the other was creeping cold.

'Oh! – I'm falling.' She turned and held me – and I sank into a smell of doughnuts.

Holding this girl was advanced stuff indeed. She was sixteen and worked in the cake shop. She was more grown-up than any girl I'd yet touched – the others had only been children. Yet suddenly, enveloped in her great bare arms, the raciness went out of the encounter, her chatter quietened to almost maternal whispers, became little sounds of content and comfort.

I forgot the cowshed and the cowshed boys. Ellie was a revol-ution – a brimming generosity heaving with uncertainties and rounder than all my imaginings. So silent now, her wordless lips to my ear, her warm breadth turned towards me, she became not an adventure but a solemn need. Even Rudolph went out of my mind. . . .

The June twilight came down and we disentangled our hair. The wall narrowed as we drew apart. Ellie's crumpled blue dress had moss in the folds like crevices filled with birds' nests.

'Look what I got,' she said, fishing behind the wall. She produced a bag full of crusty doughnuts. 'We won't need no supper. I get 'em from work. I live on 'em practically.' She gave me one and sank her teeth into another. 'You're a boy all right,' she said. 'You got a nerve.' She took another deep bite, and her teeth came out red with jam.

I couldn't forget Ellie after that, and there were vivid dreams at night, when her great brown body and crusty roundness became half girl and half groceries. My sleep knew the touch of gritty sugar on the lips and the crisp skin fresh from the bakery, enclosing who knew what stores of sweet dough, or what light dabs of jam hidden deep. . . .

I began to meet Ellie at frequent intervals, though I looked for her all the time. Perhaps a week would go by without seeing her, then she would suddenly pop up in the lane. 'Ah, there's my boy,' she'd say with a gurgle, and lead me away through the nettles. In the nests we made among the hedges, or in the quarries above the Severn, we lay innocently enough for hours together, eating each other or eating cakes.

I was oblivious now to the normal world and remote from its small affairs. Occasionally we were shadowed by some cowshed boys, but they might just as well have been sheep. Once or twice I saw Rudolph watching us sharply through a hedge, but I felt neither pity nor anger. . . .

Then one evening Ellie leaned from her moving bus and called she had something to tell me. As soon as we met, on our frontier between villages, I could see that something was up. She'd done her hair a new way, in great piled-up coils, and her smile was bulging with secrets.

She said her mum and dad had gone away for a week and left her in charge of the house. To prove it, she opened the neck of her dress and produced a door key large as a trowel. It was going to be lovely; she'd move down from the attic and sleep in the big brass bed. She'd be all by herself, just her and the cat. So I'd best not go near her, had I?

For the next couple of days I was quiet with decision, though I shook whenever I thought about it. What I had to do seemed so inevitable that I felt almost noble, like being called to war. But I took my time; I was older now, I thought I'd better not act like a savage. When the third night came, remote and still, I knew it must be the one. With the family in bed, I stole out of the house and lifted my bicycle over the gate.

I rode up the hill through waves of warm moonlight and crossed the common between our villages. I took long deep breaths, feeling heavy with destiny, going proud and melancholy to my task, wondering all the time, with salt on my tongue, whether I'd be changed when I returned this way, and thinking of the dark locked house at the end of my journey, with its enclosed and waiting girl.

Ellie's place stood alone at the edge of the village, a little way down a cart-track. It was silent, lampless, heavily loaded with moonlight and as pretty as one could wish. I buried my bicycle in a growth of nettles and crept sweating into the garden. I didn't pause for a moment to wonder what I was up to, every act seemed ordained by legend.

I saw the open window above my head and started climbing the spout towards it. A roosting bird scurried out of a gutter, but I climbed boldly, alarming nature. What would happen when I leapt light-footed into the room and confronted the sleeping girl? Would she gasp with pleasure and open her arms, cry for mercy, or lose her reason?

I reached the window, and a wave of warm air, scented with Ellie, flowed out to greet me. I straddled the sill, wriggled my way through the casement, avoided a flowerpot, and I was in.

As my feet touched the floor I saw the moonlit bed and the white breathing weight of the girl. Her bare sleeping arms were like shining rivers, her night-dress like drifts of ice, and her long dark locks, coiled loose on the pillow, were deep canyons carving the Alps. More beautiful and mysterious than ever I'd seen her, achingly remote and magic; all cockiness left me – I wanted to kneel to her then, first to worship, and then to love.

A floorboard creaked. Ellie sighed and stirred, then dreamily turned towards me.

'Oh, no!' she gurgled. 'Not *you* again, really! Rudolph, you bad, bad boy. . . .'

Starting-points

1. *Look again at each meeting the boy has with Ellie. Talk about what happens and how he feels. Write as the boy might write for his diary – an honest, personal account of each of these meetings.*

2. *The boys boast, exaggerate and lie about their experiences with the opposite sex. Talk about why they do this. Do you think girls behave in the same way?*

3. *The writer includes several comic touches in his descriptions and in the way events turn out in the story. Make a list of these, including those instances where the writer makes a joke against himself. Discuss these and decide what they add to the story.*

Suggestions for Writing

A. Look again at the boy's second meeting with Ellie when he is with Rudolph. Write the account of this meeting as Rudolph would tell it.

B. Using the notes collected for Starting-point 3, illustrate fully the writer's use of humour in the story.

THE END OF SOMETHING

Ernest Hemingway

IN the old days Hortons Bay was a lumbering town. No one who lived in it was out of sound of the big saws in the mill by the lake. Then one year there were no more logs to make lumber. The lumber schooners came into the bay and were loaded with the cut of the mill that stood stacked in the yard. All the piles of lumber were carried away. The big mill building had all its machinery that was removable taken out and hoisted on board one of the schooners by the men who had worked in the mill. The schooner moved out of the bay toward the open lake carrying the two great saws, the travelling carriage that hurled the logs against the revolving, circular saws, and all the rollers, wheels, belts, and iron piled on a hull-deep load of lumber. Its open hold covered with canvas and lashed tight, the sails of the schooner filled and it moved out into the open lake, carrying with it everything that had made the mill a mill and Hortons Bay a town.

The one-storey bunk houses, the eating-house, the company store, the mill offices, and the big mill itself stood deserted in the acres of sawdust that covered the swampy meadow by the shore of the bay.

Ten years later there was nothing of the mill left except the broken white limestone of its foundations showing through the swampy second growth as Nick and Marjorie rowed along the shore. They were trolling along the edge of the channel bank where the bottom dropped off suddenly from sandy shallows to twelve feet of dark water. They were trolling on their way to the point to set night-lines for rainbow trout.

'There's our old ruin, Nick,' Marjorie said.

Nick, rowing, looked at the white stone in the green trees.

'There it is,' he said.

'Can you remember when it was a mill?' Marjorie asked.

'I can just remember,' Nick said.

'It seems more like a castle,' Marjorie said.

Nick said nothing. They rowed on out of sight of the mill, following the shore line. Then Nick cut across the bay.

'They aren't striking,' he said.

'No,' Marjorie said. She was intent on the rod all the time they trolled, even when she talked. She loved to fish. She loved to fish with Nick.

Close beside the boat a big trout broke the surface of the water. Nick pulled hard on one oar so the boat would turn and the bait spinning far behind would pass where the trout was feeding. As the trout's back came up out of the water the minnows jumped wildly. They sprinkled the surface like a handful of shot thrown into the water. Another trout broke water, feeding on the other side of the boat.

'They're feeding,' Marjorie said.

'But they won't strike,' Nick said.

He rowed the boat around to troll past both the feeding fish, then headed it for the point. Marjorie did not reel in until the boat touched the shore.

They pulled the boat up the beach and Nick lifted out a pail of live perch. The perch swam in the water in the pail. Nick caught three of them with his hands and cut their heads off and skinned them while Marjorie chased with her hands in the bucket, finally caught a perch, cut its head off, and skinned it. Nick looked at her fish.

'You don't want to take the ventral fin out,' he said. 'It'll be all right for bait but it's better with the ventral fin in.'

He hooked each of the skinned perch through the tail. There were two hooks attached to a leader on each rod. Then Marjorie rowed the boat out over the channel-bank, holding the line in her teeth, and looking toward Nick, who stood on the shore holding the rod and letting the line run out from the reel.

'That's about right,' he called.

'Should I let it drop?' Marjorie called back, holding the line in her hand.

'Sure. Let it go.' Marjorie dropped the line overboard and watched the baits go down through the water.

She came in with the boat and ran the second line out the same way. Each time Nick set a heavy slab of driftwood across the butt of the rod to hold it solid and propped it up at an angle with a small slab. He reeled in the slack line so the line ran taut out to where the bait rested on the sandy floor of the channel and set the click on the reel. When a trout, feeding on the bottom, took the bait it would run

81

with it, taking line out of the reel in a rush and making the reel sing with the click on.

Marjorie rowed up the point a little way so she would not disturb the line. She pulled hard on the oars and the boat went way up the beach. Little waves came in with it. Marjorie stepped out of the boat and Nick pulled the boat high up the beach.

'What's the matter, Nick?' Marjorie asked.

'I don't know,' Nick said, getting wood for a fire.

They made a fire with driftwood. Marjorie went to the boat and brought a blanket. The evening breeze blew the smoke toward the point, so Marjorie spread the blanket out between the fire and the lake.

Marjorie sat on the blanket with her back to the fire and waited for Nick. He came over and sat down beside her on the blanket. In back of them was the close second-growth timber of the point and in front was the bay with the mouth of Hortons Creek. It was not quite dark. The firelight went as far as the water. They could both see the two steel rods at an angle over the dark water. The fire glinted on the reels.

Marjorie unpacked the basket of supper.

'I don't feel like eating,' said Nick.

'Come on and eat, Nick.'

'All right.'

They ate without talking, and watched the two rods and the firelight in the water.

'There's going to be a moon tonight,' said Nick. He looked across the bay to the hills that were beginning to sharpen against the sky. Beyond the hills he knew the moon was coming up.

'I know it,' Marjorie said happily.

'You know everything,' Nick said.

'Oh, Nick, please cut it out! Please, please don't be that way!'

'I can't help it,' Nick said. 'You do. You know everything. That's the trouble. You know you do.'

Marjorie did not say anything.

'I've taught you everything. You know you do. What don't you know, anyway?'

'Oh, shut up,' Marjorie said. 'There comes the moon.'

They sat on the blanket without touching each other and watched the moon rise.

'You don't have to talk silly,' Marjorie said. 'What's really the matter?'

'I don't know.'

'Of course you know.'

'No, I don't.'

'Go on and say it.'

Nick looked on at the moon, coming up over the hills.

'It isn't fun any more.'

He was afraid to look at Marjorie. Then he looked at her. She sat there with her back toward him. He looked at her back. 'It isn't fun any more. Not any of it.'

She didn't say anything. He went on. 'I feel as though everything was gone to hell inside of me. I don't know, Marge. I don't know what to say.'

He looked on at her back.

'Isn't love any fun?' Marjorie said.

'No,' Nick said. Marjorie stood up. Nick sat there, his head in his hands.

'I'm going to take the boat,' Marjorie called to him. 'You can walk back around the point.'

'All right,' Nick said. 'I'll push the boat off for you.'

'You don't need to,' she said. She was afloat in the boat on the water with the moonlight on it. Nick went back and lay down with his face in the blanket by the fire. He could hear Marjorie rowing on the water.

He lay there for a long time. He lay there while he heard Bill come into the clearing walking around through the woods. He felt Bill coming up to the fire. Bill didn't touch him, either.

'Did she go all right?' Bill said.

'Yes,' Nick said, lying, his face on the blanket.

'Have a scene?'

'No, there wasn't any scene.'

'How do you feel?'

'Oh, go away, Bill! Go away for a while.'

Bill selected a sandwich from the lunch basket and walked over to have a look at the rods.

Starting-points

1. *Look again at the conversation between Marjorie and Nick and at the writer's description of fishing. Work out from what they say and do what each is feeling. Talk about the different ways the three people in the story feel about each other.*

2. *Discuss the part Bill plays in the story. Imagine a meeting between him and Nick some time before these events begin. What would they say to each other? What would they be doing? Write the scene which comes before this story starts.*

3. *In groups of three, decide how well Nick managed his conversation with Marjorie. Work out a story in which one person has to tell another that a relationship is over. Decide who your three characters are and improvise what they say to each other. Do you think Nick was right to do what he did?*

Suggestions for Writing

A. *Give a clear and detailed account of the kind of person Marjorie is and how she behaves in the story. Or rewrite the story from her point of view so that her feelings and attitudes are clear to your reader.*

B. *Using some of the ideas collected in Starting-point 1, outline the feelings of Marjorie and Nick as the writer reveals them through the story. Show which person you have more sympathy with.*

THE DISGRACE OF JIM SCARFEDALE

Alan Sillitoe

I'M easily led and swung, my mind like a weather-vane when somebody wants to change it for me, but there's one sure rule I'll stick to for good, and I don't mind driving a nail head-first into a bloody long rigmarole of a story to tell you what I mean.

Jim Scarfedale.

I'll never let anybody try and tell me that you don't have to sling your hook as soon as you get to the age of fifteen. You ought to be able to do it earlier, only it's against the law, like everyone else in this poxetten land of hope and glory.

You see, you can't hang on to your mam's apron-strings for ever, though it's a dead cert there's many a bloke as would like to. Jim Scarfedale was one of these. He hung on so long that in the end he couldn't get used to anything else, and when he tried to change I swear blind he didn't know the difference between an apron-string and a pair of garters, though I'm sure his brand-new almost beautiful wife must have tried to drum it into his skull before she sent him whining back to his mother.

Well, I'm not going to be one of that sort. As soon as I see a way of making-off – even if I have to rob meters to feed myself – I'll take it. Instead of doing arithmetic lessons at school I glue my eyes to the atlas under my desk, planning the way I'm going to take when the time comes (with the ripped-out map folded up in my back pocket): bike to Derby, bus to Manchester, train to Glasgow, nicked car to Edinburgh, and hitch-hiking down to London. I can never stop looking at them maps, with their red roads and brown hills and marvellous other cities – so it's no wonder I can't add up for toffee. (Yes, I know, every city's the same when you come to weigh it up: the same hostels full of thieves all out to snatch your last bob if you give them half the chance; the same factories full of work, if you're lucky; the same mildewed backyards and houses full of silver-fish and black-clocks when you suddenly switch on the light at night;

85

but nevertheless, even though they're all the same they're different as well in dozens of ways, and nobody can deny it.)

Jim Scarfedale lived in our terrace, with his mam, in a house like our own, only it was a lot nearer the bike factory, smack next to it in fact, so that it was a marvel to me how they stuck it with all the noise you could hear. They might just as well have been inside the factory, because the racket it kicked up was killing. I went in the house once to tell Mrs Scarfedale that Mr Taylor at the shop wanted to see her about her week's grub order, and while I was telling her this I could hear the engines and pulleys next door in the factory thumping away, and iron-presses slamming as if they were trying to burst through the wall and set up another department at the Scarfedale's. It wouldn't surprise me a bit if it was this noise, as much as Jim's mam, that made him go the way he did.

Jim's mam was a big woman, a Tartar, a real six-footer who kept her house as clean as a new pin, and who fed Jim up to his eyeballs on steam puddings and Irish stew. She was the sort of woman as 'had a way with her' – which meant that she usually got what she wanted and knew that what she wanted was right. Her husband had coughed himself to death with consumption not long after Jim was born, and Mrs Scarfedale had set to working at the tobacco factory to earn enough for herself and Jim. She stayed hard at it for donkey's years, and she had a struggle to make ends meet through the dole days, I will say that for her, and Jim always had some sort of suit on his back every Sunday morning – which was a bloody sight more than anybody else in the terrace had. But even though he was fed more snap than the rest of us he was a small lad, and I was as big at thirteen as he was at twenty-seven (by which time it struck me that he must have stopped growing) even though I'd been half clambed to death. The war was on then – when we in our family thought we were living in the lap of luxury because we were able to stuff ourselves on date-jam and Oxo – and they didn't take Jim in the army because of his bad eyes, and his mam was glad at this because his dad had got a gob full of gas in the Great War. So Jim stayed with his mam, which I think was worse in the end than if he'd gone for a soldier and been blown to bits by the Jerries.

It worn't long after the war started that Jim surprised us all by getting married.

When he told his mam what he was going to do there was such ructions that we could hear them all the way up the yard. His mam hadn't even seen the girl, and that was what made it worse, she shouted. Courting on the sly like that and suddenly upping and saying he was getting married, without having mentioned a word of it before. Ungrateful, after all she'd done for him, bringing him up so well, even though he'd had no dad. Think of all the times she'd slaved for him! Think of it! Just think of it! (Jesus, you should have heard her.) Day in and day out she'd worked her fingers to the bone at that fag-packing machine, coming home at night dead to the wide yet cooking his dinners and mending his britches and cleaning his room out – it didn't bear thinking about. And now what had he gone and done, by way of thanks? (Robbed her purse? I asked myself quickly in the breathless interval; pawned the sheets and got drunk on the dough, drowned the cat, cut her window plants down with a pair of scissors?) No, he'd come home and told her he was getting married, just like that. It wasn't the getting married she minded – oh no, not that at all, of course it wasn't, because every young chap had to get married one day – so much as him not having brought the girl home before now for her to see and talk to. Why hadn't he done this? Was he ashamed of his mother? Didn't he think she was respectable enough to be seen by his young woman? Didn't he like to bring her back to his own home – you should have heard the way she said 'home': it made my blood run cold – even though it was cleaned every day from top to bottom? Was he ashamed of his house as well? Or was it the young woman he was ashamed of? Was she *that* sort? Well, it was a mystery, it was and all. And what's more it wasn't fair, it wasn't. Do you think it's fair, Jim? Do you? Ay, maybe you do, but I don't and I can't think of anybody else as would either.

She stopped shouting and thumping the table for a minute and then the waterworks began. Fair would you say it was – she sobbed her socks off – after all I've struggled and sweated getting you up for school every morning when you was little and sitting you down to porridge and bacon before you went out into the snow with your topcoat on, which was more than any of the other little rag-bags in the yard wore because their dads and mams boozed the dole money. (She said this, she really did, because I was listening from a place where I couldn't help but hear it – and I'll swear blind our dad never boozed a penny of his dole money and we were still clambed half to death on it. . . .) And I think of all the times when you was badly and I fetched the doctor, she went on screaming. Think of it. But I suppose you're too self-pinnyated to think, which is what my spoiling's done for you, aren't you? Eh?

The tears stopped. I think you might have had the common decency to tell me you wanted to get married and had started courting. She didn't know how he'd managed it, that she didn't, especially when she'd kept her eyes on him so well. I shouldn't have let you go twice a week to that Co-op youth club of yourn, she shouted, suddenly realising where he'd seen his chance. That was it. By God it was, that was it. And you telling me you was playing draughts and listening to blokes talk politics! Politics! That's what they called it, was it? First thing I knew. They called it summat else in my day, and it worn't such a pretty name, either. Ay, by God. And now you've got the cheek to stand there, still with your coat on, not even offering to drop all this married business. (She hadn't given him the chance to.) Why, Jim, how could you think about getting married (tap on again) when I've been so good to you? My poor lad, hasn't even realised what it's cost me and how I've worked to keep us together all these years, ever since your poor dad died. But I'll tell you one thing, my lad (tap off, sharp, and the big finger wagging), you'd better bring her to me and let me see her, and if she ain't up to much, yer can let her go and look for somebody else, if she still feels inclined.

By God, I was all of a tremble myself when I climbed down from my perch, though I wouldn't have took it like Jim did, but would have bashed her between the eyes and slung my hook there and then. Jim was earning good money and could have gone anywhere in the country, the bloody fool.

I suppose you'll be wondering how everybody in the yard knew all about what went on in Jim's house that night, and how it is that I'm able to tell word for word what Jim's mam said to him. Well, this is how it was: with Jim's house being so near the factory there's a ledge between the factory roof and his scullery window, the thickness of a double-brick wall, and I was thin-rapped enough to squeeze myself along this and listen-in. The scullery window was open, and so was the scullery door that led to the kitchen, so I heard all as went on. And nobody in the house twigged it either. I found this place out when I was eight, when I used to go monkey-climbing all over the buildings in our yard. It'd 'ave been dead easy to burgle the Scarfedale's house, except that there worn't anything much worth pinching, and except that the coppers would have jumped on me for it right away.

Well, we all knew then what went off right enough, but what surprised everybody was that Jim Scarfedale meant what he said and wasn't going to let his mam play the bully and stop him from getting married. I was on my perch the second night when sucky Jim brought his young woman to face his tub-thumping mother. She'd made him promise that much, at least.

I don't know why, but everybody in the yard expected to see some poor crumby-faced boss-eyed tart from Basford, a scruffy, half-baked, daft sort of piece that wouldn't say boo to a goose. But they got a shock. And so did I when I spied her through the scullery window. (Mrs Scarfedale was crackers about fresh air, I will say that for her.) I'd never heard anybody talk so posh, as if she'd come straight out of an office, and it made me think that Jim hadn't lied after all when he said they'd talked about politics at the club.

'Good evening, Mrs Scarfedale,' she said as she came in. There was a glint in her eye, and a way she had, that made me think she'd been born talking as posh as she did. I wondered what she saw in Jim, whether she'd found out unbeknown to any of us, that he'd been left some money, or was going to win the Irish Sweepstake. But no, Jim wasn't lucky enough for either, and I suppose his mam was thinking this at the same time as I was. Nobody shook hands.

'Sit down,' Jim's mam said. She turned to the girl, and looked at her properly for the first time, hard. 'I hear as you're wanting to marry my lad?'

'That's right, Mrs Scarfedale,' she said, taking the best chair, though sitting in it stiff and not at her ease. 'We're going to be married quite soon.' Then she tried to be more friendly, because Jim had given her the eye, like a little dog. 'My name's Phyllis Blunt. Call me Phyllis.' She looked at Jim, and Jim smiled at her because she was so nice to his mam after all. He went on smiling, as if he'd been practising all the afternoon in the lavatory mirror at the place where he worked. Phyllis smiled back, as though she'd been used to smiling like that all her life. Smiles all over the place, but it didn't mean a thing.

'What we have to do first,' Jim said, putting his foot in it, though in a nice sociable way, 'is get a ring.'

I could see the way things were going right enough. His mam suddenly went blue in the face. 'It ain't like *that*?' she brought out. 'Is it?'

She couldn't touch Phyllis with a barge-pole. 'I'm not pregnant, if that's what you mean.'

Mrs Scarfedale didn't know I was chiking, but I'll bet we both thought together: Where's the catch in it, then? Though it soon dawned on me that there wasn't any catch, at least not of the sort we must have thought of. And if this had dawned on Mrs Scarfedale at the same time as it did on me there wouldn't have been the bigger argument that night – all of them going at it worse than tigers – and perhaps poor Jim wouldn't have got married as quick as he did.

'Well,' his mother complained to our mam one day at the end of the yard about a month after they'd got spliced, 'he's made his bed, and he can lie on it, even though it turns out to be a bed of nettles, which I for one told him it was bound to be.'

Yet everybody hoped Jim would be able to keep on lying on it, because they'd always had something against such domineering strugglers as Mrs Scarfedale. Not that everybody in our yard hadn't been a struggler – and still was – one way or another. You had to be, or just lay down and die. But Jim's mam sort of carried a placard about saying: I'm a struggler but a cut above everybody else because I'm so good at it. You could tell a mile off that she was a struggler and that was what nobody liked.

She was right about her lad though. Sod it, some people said. Jim didn't lie on his bed for long, though his wife wasn't a bad-looking piece and I can see now that he should have stayed between those sheets for longer than he did. Inside six months he was back, and we all wondered what could have gone wrong – as we saw him walking down the yard carrying a suitcase and two paper bundles, looking as miserable as sin and wearing the good suit he'd got married in to save it getting creased in the case. Well, I said to myself, I'll be back on my perch soon to find out what happened between Jim and his posh missis. Yes, we'd all been expecting him to come back to his mam if you want to know the dead honest truth, even though we *hoped* he wouldn't, poor lad. Because in the first three months of his being married he'd hardly come to see her at all, and most people thought from this that he'd settled down a treat and that married life must be suiting him. But I knew different, for when a bloke's just got married he comes home often to see his mam and dad – if he's happy. That's only natural. But Jim stayed away, or tried to, and that showed me that his wife was helping all she could to stop him seeing his mam. After them first three months, though, he came home more and more often – instead of the other way round – sometimes sleeping a night, which meant that his fights with Phyllis were getting worse and worse. That last time he came he had a bandage round his napper, a trilby hat stuck on top like a lopsided crown.

I got to my perch before Jim opened his back door, and I was able to see him come in and make out what sort of a welcome his mam gave him. She was clever, I will say that for her. If she had thought about it she could have stopped his marriage a dozen times by using a bit of craft I'll bet. There was no: 'I told you so. You should have listened to me and then everything wouldn't have happened.' No, she kissed him and mashed him a cup of tea, because she knew that if she played her cards right she could have him at home for good. You could see how glad she was – could hardly stop herself smiling – as she picked up his case and parcels and carried them upstairs to his room, meaning to make his bed while the kettle boiled, leaving him a blank ten-minute sit-down in peace which she knew was just what he wanted.

But you should have seen poor old Jim, his face wicked-badly, forty-five if he looked a day, as if he'd just been let out of a Jap prisoner-of-war camp and staring – like he was crackers – at the same patch of carpet he'd stared at when he was only a kid on his pot. He'd always had a bit of a pain screwed into his mug – born that way I should think – but now it seemed as though he'd got an invisible sledge-hammer hanging all the time in front of his miserable clock ready to fall against his snout. It would have made my heart bleed if I hadn't guessed he'd been such a sodding fool, getting wed with a nice tart and then making a mess of it all.

He sat like that for a quarter of an hour, and I'll swear blind he didn't hear a single one of the homely sounds coming from upstairs, of his mam making his bed and fixing up his room, like I did. And I kept wishing she'd make haste and get done with it, but she knew what she was doing all right, dusting the mirror and polishing the pictures for her sucky lad.

Well, she came down all of a smile (trying to hide it as best she could though) and set his bread and cheese out on the table, but he didn't touch a bite, only swigged three mugs of tea straight off while she sat in her chair and looked at him as if she, anyway, would make a good supper for him.

'I'll tell you, Mam,' he began as soon as she came and set herself staring at him from the other end of the table to get him blabbing just like this. 'I've been through hell in the last six months, and I never want to go through it again.'

It was like a dam breaking down. In fact the crack in a dam wall that you see on the pictures came into his forehead just like that, exactly. And once he got started there was no holding him back. 'Tell me about it then, my lad' – though there was no need for her to have said this: he was trembling like a jelly, so that I was sometimes hard put to it to know what was going on. Honest, I can't tell it all in Jim's own words because it'd break my heart; and I really did feel sorry for him as he went on and on.

'Mam,' he moaned, dipping bread and butter in his tea, a thing I'm sure he'd never been able to do with his posh missis at the table, 'she led me a dog's life. In fact a dog would have been better off in his kennel with an old bone to chew now and again than I was with her. It was all right at first, because you see, Mam, she had some idea that a working bloke like myself was good and honest and all that sort of thing. I never knew whether she'd read this in a book or whether she'd known working blokes before that were different from me, but she might have read it because she had a few books in the house that I never looked at, and she never mentioned any other blokes in her life. She used to say that it was a treat to be able to marry and live with a bloke like me who used his bare hands for a living, because there weren't many blokes in the world, when you considered it, who did good hard labouring work. She said she'd die if ever she married a bloke as worked in an office and who crawled around his boss because he wanted to get on. So I thought it would go off all right, Mam, honest I did, when she said nice things like this to me. It made the netting factory look better to me, and I didn't so much mind carrying bobbins from one machine to another. I was happy with her and I thought that she was happy with me. At first she made a bigger fuss of me than before we were married even, and when I came home at night she used to talk about politics and books and things, saying how the world was made for blokes like me and that we should run the world and not leave it to a lot of money-grubbing capitalist bastards who didn't know any more about it than to talk like babies week after week and get nothing done that was any good to anybody.

'But to tell you the truth, Mam, I was too tired to talk politics after I'd done a hard day's graft, and then she started to ask questions, and would get ratty after a while when she began to see that I couldn't answer what she wanted to know. She asked me all sorts of things, about my bringing up, about my dad, about all the neighbours in the terrace, but I could never tell her much, anyway, not what she wanted to know, and that started a bit of trouble. At first she packed my lunches and dinners and there was always a nice hot tea and some clothes to change into waiting for me when I came home, but later on she wanted me to have a bath every night, and that caused a bit of trouble because I was too tired to have a bath and often I was too fagged out even to change my clothes. I wanted to sit in my overalls listening to the wireless and reading the paper in peace. Once when I was reading the paper and she was getting mad because I couldn't get my eyes off the football results she put a match to the bottom of the paper and I didn't know about it till the flames almost came into my face. I got a fright, I can tell you, because

I thought we were still happy then. And she made a joke about it, and even went out to buy me another newspaper, so I thought it was all right and that it was only a rum joke she'd played. But not long after that when I'd got the racing on the wireless she said she couldn't stand the noise and that I should listen to something better, so she pulled the plug out and wouldn't put it back.

'Yes, she did very well by me at first, that I will say, just like you, Mam, but then she grew tired of it all, and started to read books all day, and there'd be nowt on the table at tea-time when I came home dead to the wide except a packet of fags and a bag of toffees. She was all loving to me at first, but then she got sarcastic and said she couldn't stand the sight of me. "Here comes the noble savage," she called out when I came home, and used longer words I didn't know the meaning of when I asked her where my tea was. "Get it yourself," she said, and one day when I picked up one of her toffees from the table she threw the poker at me. I said I was hungry, but she just told me, "Well, if you are, then crawl under the table to me and I'll give you something." Honest, Mam, I can't tell you one half of what went on, because you wouldn't want to hear it.'

(Not much, I thought. I could see her as large as life licking her chops.)

'Tell me it all, my lad,' she said. 'Get it off your chest. I can see you've had a lot to put up with.'

'I did and all,' he said. 'The names she called me, Mam. It made my hair stand on end. I never thought she was that sort, but I soon found out. She used to sit in front of the fire with nothing on, and when I said that she should get dressed in case a neighbour knocked at the door, she said she was only warming her meal-ticket that the noble savage had given her, and then she'd laugh, Mam, in a way that made me so's I couldn't move. I had to get out when she carried on like that because I knew that if I stayed in she'd throw something and do damage.

'I don't know where she is now. She packed up and took her things, saying she never wanted to see me again, that I could chuck myself in the canal for all she cared. She used to shout a lot about going down to London and seeing some real life, so I suppose that's where she's gone. There was four pounds ten and threepence in a jam-jar on the kitchen shelf and when she'd gone that was gone as well.

'So I don't know, our mam, about anything, or what I'm going to do. I'd like to live here again with you if you'll have me. I'll pay you two quid a week regular for my board, and see you right. I can't put

93

up with any of that any more because I can't stand it, and I don't suppose I'll ever leave home again after all that little lot of trouble. So if you'll have me back, Mam, I'll be ever so glad. I'll work hard for you, that I will, and you'll never have to worry again. I'll do right by you and pay you back a bit for all the struggle you had in bringing me up. I heard at work the other day as I'm to have a ten-bob rise next week, so if you let me stay I'll get a new wireless and pay the deposit on it. So let me stay, our mam, because, I tell you, I've suffered a lot.'

And the way she kissed him made me sick, so I got down from my monkey-perch.

Jim Scarfedale stayed, right enough, the great big baby. He was never happier in his life after getting the O.K. from his old woman. All his worries were over, he'd swear blind they were, even if you tried to tell him what a daft sod he was for not packing his shaving tackle and getting out, which I did try to tell him, only he thought I was cracked even more than he was himself, I suppose. His mother thought she'd got him back for good, though, and so did we all, but we were off the mark by a mile. If you weren't stone-blind you could see he was never the same old Jim after he'd been married: he got broody and never spoke to a soul, and nobody, not even his mam, could ever get out of him where he went to every night. His face went pudgy-white and his sandy mouse-hair fell out so much that he was nearly bald in six months. Even the few freckles he had went pale. He used to slink back from wherever he'd been at twelve o'clock, whether the night was winter or summer, and never a bloke would know what he got up to. And if you asked him right out loud, like as if you were cracking a bit of a joke, 'Where you been, Jim?' he'd make as if he hadn't heard a sound.

It must have been a couple of years later when the copper came up our yard one moonlight night: I saw him from my bedroom window. He turned the corner, and I dodged back before he could spot me. You're in for it now, I said to myself, ripping lead from that empty house on Buckingham Street. You should have had more sense, you daft bogger (frightened to death I was, though I don't know why now), especially when you only got three and a tanner for it from Cooky. I always said you'd end up in Borstal, and here comes the copper to get you.

Even when he went on past our house I thought it was only because he'd got mixed up in the numbers and that he'd swing back at any minute. But no, it was the Scarfedales' door he wanted, and I'd never known a happier feeling than when I heard that rap-rap-rapping and knew that this time they hadn't come for me. Never again, I sang to myself, never again – so happy that I got the stitch – they can keep their bleeding lead.

Jim's mam screamed as soon as the copper mentioned her name. Even from where I was I heard her say, 'He's never gone and got run over, has he?'

Then I could hear no more, but a minute later she walked up the yard with the copper, and I saw her phizzog by the lamplight, looking set hard like granite, as if she would fall down and kick the bucket if you as much as whispered a word to her. The copper had to hold her arm.

It all came out next morning – the queerest case the yard had ever known. Blokes had been put inside for burglary, deserting, setting fire to buildings, bad language, being blind drunk, grabbing hold of grown women and trying to give them what-for, not paying main- tenance money, running up big debts for wirelesses and washing- machines and then selling them, poaching, trespassing, driving off in cars that didn't belong to them, trying to commit suicide, attempted murder, assault and battery, snatching handbags, shop- lifting, fraud, forgery, pilfering from work, bashing each other about, and all sorts of larks that didn't mean much. But Jim did something I hadn't heard about before, at least not in our yard.

He'd been at it for months as well, taking a bus four miles across town to places where nobody knew him and waiting in old dark streets near some lit-up beer-off for little girls of ten and eleven to come walking along carrying jugs to get their dads a pint in. And sucky Jim would jump out of his hiding-place near pieces of waste- ground and frighten the life out of them and get up to his dirty tricks. I can't understand why he did it, I can't, I really can't, but did it he did, and got copped for it as well. He did it so often that somebody must have sprung a trap, because one hard-luck night they collared him and he was put inside for eighteen months. You should have heard the telling-off he got from the judge. I'll bet the poor sod didn't know where to put his face, though I'm sure there's many a judge that's done the same, if not worse, than Jim. 'We've got to put you in clink,' the judge said, 'not only for the good of little girls but for your own good as well. People have got to be protected from the likes of you, you dirty sod.'

After that we never saw him again in our yard, because by the time he came out his mother had got a house and a new job in Derby, so's they could settle down where nobody knew them I suppose. Jim was the only bloke in our yard that ever got a big spread in *all* the newspapers, as far as I can remember, and nobody would have thought he had it in him, though I think it was a bit like cheating, getting in on them with a thing like that.

Which is why I think nobody should hang on to his mother's apron-strings for such a long time like Jim did, or they might go the same way. And that's why I look at that atlas under my desk at school instead of doing sums (up through Derbyshire and into Manchester, then up to Glasgow, across to Edinburgh, and down again to London, saying hello to Mam and Dad on the way) because I hate doing sums, especially when I think I can already reckon up all the money I'm ever likely to scoop from any small-time gas meter.

Starting-points

1. *Talk about the kind of person that Mrs Scarfedale is. How does she try to keep Jim dependent on her? Why does she do this? Do you agree that Jim's problem was that he was tied to his mother's apron-strings? Discuss what you feel about children becoming independent of their parents. Should parents encourage this process? How do your views compare with Mrs Scarfedale's?*

2. *How exactly does Jim try to stand up to his mother? Why does he fail? Talk about a time you stood up to people, successfully or otherwise.*

3. *In threes, work out a brief scene in a marriage guidance counsellor's office. A husband and wife – one middle class, the other working class – have come for advice on their problems. They each give their story, then the counsellor offers advice. Decide whether Jim and Phyllis could have been helped in this way.*

Suggestions for Writing

A. *What kind of person is the youth who tells the story? What are his attitudes and what makes him as he is? How fair is he to Jim and to his mother?*

B. *As if you were perched on a ledge outside, describe the scene when Jim comes home fagged out and his new wife sets fire to his paper. Exactly what kind of husband was Phyllis looking for?*

GROWING UP

Joyce Cary

ROBERT QUICK, coming home after a business trip, found a note from his wife. She would be back at four, but the children were in the garden. He tossed down his hat, and still in his dark business suit, which he disliked very much, made at once for the garden.

He had missed his two small girls and looked forward eagerly to their greeting. He had hoped indeed that they might, as often before, have been waiting at the corner of the road, to flag the car, and drive home with him.

The Quicks' garden was a wilderness. Except for a small vegetable patch near the pond, and one bed where Mrs Quick grew flowers for the house, it had not been touched for years. Old apple trees tottered over seedy laurels, unpruned roses. Tall ruins of dahlias and delphiniums hung from broken sticks.

The original excuse for this neglect was that the garden was for the children. They should do what they liked there. The original truth was that neither of the Quicks cared for gardening. Besides, Mrs Quick was too busy with family, council, and parish affairs, Quick with his office, to give time to a hobby that bored them both.

But the excuse had become true. The garden belonged to the children, and Quick was even proud of it. He would boast of his wild garden, so different from any neighbour's shaved grass and combed beds. It had come to seem, for him, a triumph of imagination; and this afternoon, once more, he found it charming in its wildness, an original masterpiece among gardens.

And, in fact, with the sun just warming up in mid-May, slanting steeply past the trees, and making even old weeds shine red and gold, it had the special beauty of untouched woods, where there is still, even among closely farmed lands, a little piece of free nature left, a suggestion of the frontier, primeval forests.

A bit of real wild country, thought Quick, a townsman for whom the country was a place for picnics. And he felt at once released, escaped. He shouted, 'Hullo, hullo, children.'

97

There was no answer. And he stopped, in surprise. Then he thought, They've gone to meet me – I've missed them. And this gave him both pleasure and dismay. The last time the children had missed him, two years before, having gone a mile down the road and lain in ambush behind a hedge, there had been tears. They had resented being searched for, and brought home; they had hated the humiliating failure of their surprise.

But even as he turned back towards the house, and dodged a tree, he caught sight of Jenny, lying on her stomach by the pond, with a book under her nose. Jenny was twelve and had lately taken furiously to reading.

Quick made for the pond with long steps, calling, 'Hullo, hullo, Jenny, hullo', waving. But Jenny merely turned her head slightly and peered at him through her hair. Then she dropped her cheek on the book as if to say, 'Excuse me, it's really too hot.'

And now he saw Kate, a year older. She was sitting on the swing, leaning sideways against a rope, with her head down, apparently in deep thought. Her bare legs, blotched with mud, lay along the ground, one foot hooked over the other. Her whole air was one of languor and concentration. To her father's 'Hullo' she answered only in a faint muffled voice, 'Hullo, Daddy'.

'Hullo, Kate.' But he said no more and did not go near. Quick never asked for affection from his girls. He despised fathers who flirted with their daughters, who encouraged them to love. It would have been especially wrong, he thought, with these two. They were naturally impulsive and affectionate – Jenny had moods of passionate devotion, especially in the last months. She was growing up, he thought, more quickly than Kate and she was going to be an exciting woman, strong in all her feelings, intelligent, reflective. 'Well, Jenny,' he said, 'what are you reading now?' But the child answered only by a slight wriggle of her behind.

Quick was amused at his own disappointment. He said to himself: 'Children have no manners but at least they're honest – they never pretend.' He fetched himself a deck-chair and the morning paper, which he had hardly looked at before his early start on the road. He would make the best of things. At fifty-two, having lost most of his illusions, he was good at making the best of things. It's a lovely day, he thought, and I'm free till Sunday night. He looked round him as he opened the paper and felt again the pleasure of the garden. What a joy, at last, to be at peace. And the mere presence of the children was a pleasure. Nothing could deprive him of that. He was home again.

Jenny had got up and wandered away among the trees; her legs too were bare and dirty, and her dress had a large green stain at the side. She had been in the pond. And now Kate allowed herself to collapse slowly out of the swing and lay on her back with her hair tousled in the dirt, her arms thrown apart, her small dirty hands with black nails turned palm upwards to the sky. Her cocker bitch, Snort, came loping and sniffing, uttered one short bark and rooted at her mistress's legs. Kate raised one foot and tickled her stomach, then rolled over and buried her face in her arms. When Snort tried to push her nose under Kate's thigh as if to turn her over, she made a half kick and murmured, 'Go away, Snort.'

'Stop it, Snort,' Jenny echoed in the same meditative tone. The sisters adored each other and one always came to the other's help. But Snort only stopped a moment to gaze at Jenny, then tugged at Kate's dress. Kate made another more energetic kick and said, 'Oh, do go away, Snort.'

Jenny stopped in her languid stroll, snatched a bamboo from the border, and hurled it at Snort like a spear.

The bitch, startled, uttered a loud uncertain bark and approached, wagging her behind so vigorously that she curled her body sideways at each wag. She was not sure if this was a new game, or if she had committed some grave crime. Jenny gave a yell and rushed at her. She fled yelping. At once Kate jumped up, seized another bamboo and threw it, shouting, 'Tiger, tiger.'

The two children dashed after the bitch, laughing, bumping together, falling over each other and snatching up anything they could find to throw at the fugitive, pebbles, dead daffodils, bits of flowerpots, lumps of earth. Snort, horrified, overwhelmed, dodged to and fro, barked hysterically, crazily, wagged her tail in desperate submission; finally put it between her legs and crept whining between a broken shed and the wall.

Robert was shocked. He was fond of the sentimental foolish Snort, and he saw her acute misery. He called to the children urgently, 'Hi, Jenny – don't do that. Don't do that, Kate. She's frightened – you might put her eye out. Hi, stop – stop.'

This last cry expressed real indignation. Jenny had got hold of a rake and was trying to hook Snort by the collar. Robert began to struggle out of his chair. But suddenly Kate turned round, aimed a pea-stick at him and shouted at the top of her voice, 'Yield, Paleface.' Jenny at once turned and cried, 'Yes, yes – Paleface, yield.' She burst into a shout of laughter and could not speak, but rushed at the man with the rake carried like a lance.

The two girls, staggering with laughter, threw themselves upon their father. 'Paleface – Paleface Robbie. Kill him – scalp him. Torture him.'

They tore at the man and suddenly he was frightened. It seemed to him that both the children, usually so gentle, so affectionate, had gone completely mad, vindictive. They were hurting him, and he did not know how to defend himself without hurting them, without breaking their skinny bones, which seemed as fragile as a bird's legs. He dared not even push too hard against the thin ribs which seemed to bend under his hand. Snort, suddenly recovering confidence, rushed barking from cover and seized this new victim by the sleeve, grunting and tugging.

'Hi,' he shouted, trying to catch at the bitch. 'Call her off, Kate. Don't, don't, children.' But they battered at him, Kate was jumping on his stomach, Jenny had seized him by the collar as if to strangle him. Her face, close to his own, was that of a homicidal maniac; her eyes were wide and glaring, her lips were curled back to show all her teeth. And he was really strangling. He made a violent effort to throw the child off, but her hands were firmly twined in his collar. He felt his ears sing. Then suddenly the chair gave way – all three fell with a crash. Snort, startled, and perhaps pinched, gave a yelp, and snapped at the man's face.

Kate was lying across his legs, Jenny on his chest; she still held his collar in both hands. But now, gazing down at him, her expression changed. She cried, 'Oh, she's bitten you. Look, Kate.' Kate, rolling off his legs, came to her knees, 'So she has, bad Snort.'

The girls were still panting, flushed, struggling with laughter. But Jenny reproached her sister, 'It's not a joke. It might be poisoned.'

'I know.' Kate was indignant. But burst out again into helpless giggles.

Robert picked himself up and dusted his coat. He did not utter any reproaches. He avoided even looking at the girls in case they should see his anger and surprise. He was deeply shocked. He could not forget Jenny's face, crazy, murderous; he thought: Not much affection there – she wanted to hurt. It was as if she hated me.

It seemed to him that something new had broken into his old simple and happy relation with his daughters; that they had suddenly receded from him into a world of their own in which he had no standing, a primitive, brutal world.

He straightened his tie. Kate had disappeared; Jenny was gazing at his forehead and trying to suppress her own giggles. But when he turned away, she caught his arm, 'Oh Daddy, where are you going?'

'To meet your mother – she must be on her way.'

'Oh, but you can't go like that – we've got to wash your bite.'

'That's all right, Jenny. It doesn't matter.'

'But Kate is getting the water – and it might be quite bad.'

And now, Kate, coming from the kitchen with a bowl of water, called out indignantly, 'Sit down, Daddy – sit down – how dare you get up.'

She was playing the stern nurse. And in fact, Robert, though still in a mood of disgust, found himself obliged to submit to this new game. At least it was more like a game. It was not murderous. And a man so plump and bald could not allow himself even to appear upset by the roughness of children. Even though the children would not understand why he was upset, why he was shocked.

'Sit down at once, man,' Jenny said. 'Kate, put up the chair.'

Kate put up the chair, the two girls made him sit down, washed the cut, painted it with iodine, stuck a piece of plaster on it. Mrs Quick, handsome, rosy, good-natured, practical, arrived in the middle of this ceremony, with her friend Jane Martin, Chairman of the Welfare Committee. Both were much amused by the scene, and the history of the afternoon. Their air said plainly to Robert, 'All you children – amusing yourselves while we run the world.'

Kate and Jenny were sent to wash and change their dirty frocks. The committee was coming to tea. And at tea, the two girls, dressed in smart clean frocks, handed round cake and bread and butter with demure and reserved looks. They knew how to behave at tea, at a party. They were enjoying the dignity of their own performance. Their eyes passed over their father as if he did not exist, or rather as if he existed only as another guest, to be waited on.

And now, seeking as it were a new if lower level of security, of resignation, he said to himself, 'Heavens, but what did I expect? In a year or two more I shan't count at all. Young men will come prowling, like the dogs after Snort – I shall be an old buffer, useful only to pay bills.'

The ladies were talking together about a case – the case of a boy of fourteen, a nice respectable boy, most regular at Sunday school, who had suddenly robbed his mother's till and gone off in a stolen car. Jenny, seated at her mother's feet, was listening intently, Kate was feeding chocolate-roll to Snort, and tickling her chin.

Quick felt all at once a sense of stuffiness. He wanted urgently to get away, to escape. Yes, he needed some male society. He would go to the club. Probably no one would be there but the card-room crowd, and he could not bear cards. But he might find old Wilkins in the billiard room. Wilkins at seventy was a crashing, a dreary bore, who spent half his life at the club; who was always telling you how he had foreseen the slump, and how clever he was at investing his money. What good was money to old Wilkins? But, Quick thought, he could get up a game with Wilkins, pass an hour or two with him, till dinner-time, even dine with him. He could phone his wife. She would not mind. She rather liked a free evening for her various accounts. And he need not go home till the children were in bed.

And when, after tea, the committee members pulled out their agenda, he stole away. Suddenly, as he turned by the corner house, skirting its front garden wall, he heard running steps and a breathless call. He turned, it was Jenny. She arrived, panting, holding herself by the chest. 'Oh, I couldn't catch you.'

'What is it now, Jenny?'

'I wanted to look – at the cut.'

Robert began to stoop. But she cried, 'No, I'll get on the wall. Put me up.'

He lifted her on the garden wall which made her about a foot taller than himself. Having reached this superior position, she poked the plaster.

'I just wanted to make sure it was sticking. Yes, it's all right.'

She looked down at him with an expression he did not recognise. What was the game, medical, maternal? Was she going to laugh? But the child frowned. She was also struck by something new and unexpected.

Then she tossed back her hair. 'Goodbye.' She jumped down and ran off. The man walked slowly towards the club. No, he thought, not quite a game – not for half a second. She's growing up – and so am I.

Starting-points

1. *Working in pairs, develop the conversation that Jenny might have had with her mother after the events of this day. Then improvise the talk between a mother and teen-age daughter, or a father and son, where the adult is hurt by something the adolescent says or does.*

2. *In small groups, talk about the events of the story and how they change Robert Quick's relationship with his daughters. Then discuss the following questions:*

   (a) *Do you agree with Robert Quick that adults should not openly show affection to children nor encourage them to express it?*
   (b) *Should people always show others what their real feelings are?*
   (c) *Is becoming adult just a matter of making the best of things?*

3. *Robert Quick says he is still growing up. What makes him say this? Decide whether it is possible for adults to be growing up still.*

Suggestions for Writing

A. *Write a detailed study of Jenny and what she does in the story. Why does she behave as she does? Or write a version of the story told from Jenny's point of view.*

B. *Robert Quick suddenly finds the world of children primitive and brutal. Consider times when you have found the world of adults painful, frightening or shutting you out. Write a short story about one of these incidents.*

SOME GENERAL ASSIGNMENTS

1. Outline briefly the events of any *one* story that in your opinion conveys excitement in its narrative. Then examine the story closely and show how the writer, by skilful use of language, has made the story exciting.

2. Compare and contrast the ways in which the writers treat adults in any *two* stories.

3. What insights have you gained into the problems of adolescence from reading any *three* of these stories?

4. Choose *one* of the stories in this selection which has appealed to you for reasons other than the interest of the narrative itself. By close reference to your chosen story, show what it is that has appealed to you.

5. Some stories present feelings and ideas that we are already familiar with; others express a totally new idea or experience. From the stories you have read, choose *one* which presents an idea which was new to you and *one* which deals with the familiar. Show fully why it is you have chosen each example.

6. Choose *one* story which has impressed you for its power of vivid and dramatic writing and *one* which reveals the unpleasant as well as the pleasant aspects of its characters. Carefully illustrate the quality for which you have chosen each story.

7. 'Many of these authors are successful in making powerful comments about growing up even though their stories deal with ordinary people and with incidents that may seem trivial at first sight.' Illustrate this statement by careful reference to any *two* stories.

8. Choose *one* story which deals with a humorous or a dangerous situation. Give a clear picture of the situation and show how the writer has been successful in making the comedy or danger vividly realistic to the reader.